RHIANNON GRANT

Carving a New Shape

LESBIAN LOVE IN NEOLITHIC ORKNEY

Carving a New Shape Copyright © 2023 by Rhiannon Grant.

All rights reserved.
No part of this book may be used or reproduced elsewhere without written permission except in the case of brief quotations embodied in critical articles or reviews.

Publisher: Rhiannon Grant.

For information: rhiannon.bookgeek@gmail.com

For more about my work and books, including to get updates by email: brigidfoxandbuddha.wordpress.com

Book and Cover design by Rhiannon Grant
ISBN: 978-1-7395938-2-7
First Edition: September 2023

10 9 8 7 6 5 4 3 2 1

For my beloved, Piangfan Angela Grant Naksukpaiboon.

Chapter 1

THE BOAT WAS ALMOST READY. Laki stroked the side where she had helped Heln to put the finishing touches on the waterproof layer of seal fat. A little of the oil came off on her hand and she tried to wipe it back on before they lifted the boat over the rocky part of the shore, down to the sand, and into the water.

It was a calm spring day, at least at sea. Some little waves broke into soft white bubbles as they reached the beach, and the wind was gentle.

The people were a different matter. "Here," Marko said, handing Laki a leather bag full of heavy things which clinked together as it moved. She was pulled away from her contemplations and into the hurried movement: up and down the beach, loading the boat with skins and string and smoked meat and pots and more bags of stone axe-heads and other tools. Laki walked three trips carrying stuff, and then she noticed Heln had stopped and was talking quietly but intensely to eir aunt Aleuks. Laki thought that was a good enough reason for her to stop working as well. Instead, she "dropped" a bundle of furs close enough to hear some of the conversation, but behind Aleuks, who was most likely to notice what she was doing, and bent to "retie" them.

"Remember to oil..."

"... all the skins regularly." Heln sounded like ey was smiling. "Aleuks, I sailed with you for a long time. I've known this boat for a long time. I'll oil the skins, I'll check the oars, I'll watch for rocks, I'll check the stars and the clouds, I'll only set out when it's safe. I know what to do."

"I know you do." Aleuks sighed. "Sorry, Heln, I know you know what to do. But..."

"You'll miss the boat."

"And you, I'll miss you. We all will. And Marko and Laki and Sal."

It was Heln's turn to say softly, "I know. I know you will. But we'll be home in the autumn, if not before."

Laki thought it was strange to hear Heln, who had been born many months of travel to the south and only arrived in Otter Village in a storm two years ago, describe the place as eir home. But ey and Aleuks both spoke that way these days.

Aleuks was talking again but Laki missed it because a pair of feet stopped in front of her. "Do you need any help?" their owner asked. Laki looked up to find Trebbi, village leader and Aleuks's partner, standing there. She hastily tucked in a leather thong on the bundle and stood up.

"No, I'm fine. This slipped out and I need to retie it."

Trebbi nodded. Laki hefted the bundle. "Have a good journey, Laki," Trebbi said softly.

"Thank you."

"I hope you find what you're looking for."

Laki shrugged, because she didn't know what that would be. All she knew was that she needed to get away from Otter Village, discover the world, forget her loss, take control of her life, and become a new person. It was a lot to ask of a single trading voyage. "Yeah," she said to Trebbi.

"Better get that down to the boat," Trebbi replied, and Laki hurried off with her roll of furs.

Once the trading goods were loaded, the crew of four climbed in—wet feet but no accidents— and they were almost off. Aleuks stood in the surf holding the prow and for a moment Laki thought she was going to join them.

"Goddess bless you on your travels," Trebbi said in her formal–declarations voice. "*We*," she laid a hand on Aleuks's arm, "will see you in the autumn, or before."

"Goddess bless the village," Heln replied. "Have a good summer and we'll see you in a few full moons." Ey glared at Aleuks until she let go of the boat. "Oars down!"

They had practiced this and although the manoeuvre away from shore and out of the bay was a little tricky, it went smoothly.

*

The first two days were all about the rowing. The breeze from the first morning died down at midday, and by the afternoon they were only moving when they put their oars to work. Heln quizzed them all about whether there was somewhere close by they could usefully stop.

There were shrugs all round. They were still close to Otter Village, really. "I can walk to that headland," Laki said, pointing. "There isn't another village on this side. Sometimes we come over this way for the gull's eggs."

To prove her point, a couple of seagulls streaked overhead, screeching. "They think we're fishing and they might get some," Heln noted, "but I don't really want to go ashore here if there's nobody but gulls to meet."

"Let's row, then," Marko said. "And the tricky currents in the middle of the islands might be easier if there's not much wind."

They rowed until their arms could hardly move that day and the next. Heln's original plan had been to stop at the big villages around the stone circles where a boat could come into the sheltered waters. But at the crucial moment when they'd expected to turn north, the wind was blowing the wrong way. "We'll explore somewhere new," Heln decided, and with that they found themselves exploring the western coast of the islands.

*

"We need to get on with this," Klamro muttered only loud enough for Bokka to hear.

By the hearth, Genu was trying to keep everyone's attention, but Nerto's radical proposal that they not build a tomb at all and use the time for something else had succeeded in scaring the cows. The meeting, meant to be quiet and orderly and always somewhat inclined to chit–chat, was well and truly out of control as everyone debated Bokka's parent's idea at full volume.

By her side, Bokka's other parent didn't sound like ey were happy with this turn of events. "'Do something else,' indeed. And what will we do when someone dies? It happens. It happens in the winter when you can't simply nip out to build a quick tomb. Then we'd have to return them to the sea and that's not the done thing these days. All the other villages have got tombs now. We're falling behind." Klamro was not speaking loud enough for anyone else to hear.

Bokka gave a deep sigh to let em know ey had been heard. She personally didn't agree with either of her parents. She didn't really care about any of it. She was at the meeting because this was the house where the fire was lit and the food was cooking, but after she'd eaten, she was planning to go and work on a stone ball she was decorating.

"Wait, wait," Genu was saying. Bokka could hardly see him between all the other people.

"Wait for what?" Nerto asked. Twenty more conversations started at once. Ey was having a good time. Bokka imagined the crowd like fish in Nerto's net. Genu was a big, shiny fish flopping around, and soon he would die, Nerto would have him thrown back into the water. Bokka supposed that was why Genu was so keen to get a tomb built.

When he got some quiet—not silence, Bokka could still hear muttering, but enough quiet to be heard by most of the people—Genu started describing different types of tombs. Apparently if they did decide to build a tomb, they had to choose between two building styles. Genu spoke as if the first part of the decision, to build a tomb at all, was already taken. Bokka wondered if he was hungry, too, or if all this about tombs meant he didn't need to eat.

"You have to make spaces inside the tomb for different people or different families," he explained, "like we build different spaces inside our houses: a space for sleeping, a space for storing live shellfish, a space for storing cooking pots."

Bokka imagined a human body stored on a stone shelf like the ones that kept cooking pots in her parents' house. It would have to be much bigger, but it would sort of work. A bed–shaped space would be more practical.

"One style of tomb makes the spaces like houses," Genu continued. "There's a round tomb with round spaces built into the walls. It's as if our whole village was moved into the tomb, roofed over like our tunnels, and the spaces in the walls are the houses for different families."

"Does your body get put with the family you were born into, or the family you live with?" Klamro asked.

It seemed like a good question to Bokka because unless you split up the different bones and put them in more than one place, you were going to have to choose, and what if you'd moved from another village? Did you have to go back to their tomb?

Genu glared. He didn't seem to think it was a good question. "The family you're with when you die," he said, which didn't make any sense, because they were the people who were still alive.

Bokka did not ask any of her questions. She kept her eyes on the pieces of meat roasting over the fire. Genu's daughter, Pru, was turning them from time to time, and the smell was making Bokka's mouth water.

"The other style of tomb has a long space like a boat, and is divided into different family spaces with upright stones, like the sides of a bed," Genu went on. "The advantage of this is that you can make lots more divisions and..."

"Food's ready," Pru said, with a complete disregard for whatever her father was about to say.

Apparently, nobody else was very interested either. There was an immediate movement towards the fire and before long, everyone was eating fresh bread baked on hot stones, roast from the deer Nerto shot yesterday, and the spring's fresh greens, which Pru had gathered in the forest and along the shore. Bokka helped herself to plenty before finding a space at the back of the room where she hoped to sit and eat in peace.

No such luck. Nerto sat down next to eir daughter, and Nerto's best friend Noma joined them. "Did you have a good day with the sheep?" Noma asked. She was one of those task–focussed people the village really liked because she was good at planning and farming, but she annoyed Bokka. One day with the sheep was much like another. They were born and limped and ate and shed their wool and were killed and eaten. What did it matter? The important things in life were carvings and stories and maybe even tombs, but not sheep.
Noma was still looking at her, so Bokka shrugged and bit deeply into her piece of roast meat.

*

From the boat, their first view of Cow Village was of a mound green with grass on the outer edges, then white and grey, then green again where the turf roofed the houses.

"They live underground," Sal said wonderingly.

"Not really," Heln said, and Laki remembered that ey'd been before, last summer. "They've built piles of shells up around their houses to protect themselves from winter storms, but the houses started out above the ground."

"Oh." Sal shrugged and turned back to his oar.

"Best get to shore, anyway," Marko encouraged them.

Laki's arms were aching because they'd been rowing since dawn, but she pulled as hard as she could. She wanted to see inside the half–underground houses for herself.

After the initial muddle of introductions to Genu the village leader and a dozen other people whose names she couldn't remember, Laki found herself unsure what to do. The other three new arrivals were deep in conversation, but she didn't have anything to add. Instead of trying to think of something, or standing around doing nothing, she started to unload the boat. Each bag had to be carried out from the shallow water and up the beach to above the line of seaweed which marked the highest point the tide would reach. None of the individual bags were particularly heavy. It just took time.

Heln noticed what she was doing—she knew because ey gave Laki a smile—but ey got immediately drawn back into conversation about something or other and didn't yet come to help.

After dropping her fifth load high up on the beach, almost at the entrance to the village, Laki paused to take some deep breaths and look around. She noticed someone else who wasn't in the huddle of talkers. Further up the beach there was a rocky area, and a person was hunched over them, tapping something with a hammer stone. Collecting limpets, Laki guessed, and maybe observing the new arrivals from a safe distance. It was where she might have been if this were her home village.

"That's Bokka," someone said. Laki spun round. While she had been staring off into the distance, Sal and one of the people from Cow Village had followed her example and started carrying some bags up the beach. "I'm Pru," this person went on, putting down the bag she'd been carrying, "and over there, ignoring all of us, is Bokka."

Laki nodded. She wasn't sure if Bokka was actually ignoring them—why pick that exact moment to collect limpets unless it was a very strange coincidence or you wanted to be close enough to see what was happening on the beach?—but she took the point. She introduced herself to Pru. "And have you always lived in Cow Village?"

Pru was nodding, too. "My father, Genu, is our leader, and I was born here. And I love your necklace, by the way!"

Laki normally forgot about it while she was wearing it and reached up to use her fingertips to remind herself. She had made most of it the summer before, while the days were long and her mother was dying slowly. Working the whale teeth and the bone had been something to do with her hands when there was nothing

10

else she could do to help. "Thank you." She smiled, but she knew her sadness would also show.

Fortunately, Pru sensed something and changed the subject again. "Have you always been a trader?"

Laughing, Laki shook her head. "No, I was born in Otter Village and I'd never been further than round to the wooden circle where we trade with the next village. Heln is the trader here—ey came with eir aunt the winter before last, from somewhere a long way south of here."

"Interesting." Pru looked over at the two new arrivals who were still chatting.

"Ey's taken, though," Laki added, reading Pru's interest as a romantic one. "Heln and Marko are together."

"I see." Pru nodded thoughtfully and didn't stop watching Heln. "Will you be staying for long? Do you think there'll be room in the boat for more people when you leave?"

"We'll stay for as long as we need to, to trade and talk," Sal said, coming up on Pru's other side. "As for space in the boat, it's hard to know."

"My father probably wouldn't let me go with you anyway." Pru sighed. "Well, do you need any more help carrying things? This all looks very exciting!"

*

Properly arriving in Cow Village took the rest of the day. Pru gave them a tour, showing them the entrances to the half-buried houses, explaining how they built up their empty limpet shells and other rubbish around the place to provide layers of protection from the wind and the rain and the sea. Tonight, though, it was spring, and they would cook at a shared hearth at the edge of the fields in honour of their guests.

While they waited, Genu started to explain the decision the village were making about their new tomb.

"I helped to build ours," Sal said.

Laki turned to look at him. She hadn't realised Sal had been involved in that; the tomb had been built before she was born while her mother was still young, and although she'd heard some stories, it suddenly made Sal seem older than she'd previously thought.

Noticing her look, Sal smiled. "I've seen a lot of summers. My wife was one of the first people buried in the new tomb in Otter Village. I think she might have wanted to be taken into the forest, the way her family traditionally did it, but we'd worked so hard bringing the stones for the tomb. I wanted her to have the best and be with people she'd known in life."

"Tell me about your tomb," Genu demanded and launched into a discussion of the technicalities of different tomb designs. Having never been inside any of them, Laki found it difficult to follow. Instead, her eyes went to someone she recognised.

The woman, Bokka, who had been collecting limpets on the shore, was similarly on the edge of this gathering. Most of the group were sitting or squatting around the fire. They were close enough to talk to each other easily and close enough to the fire to lean in and cut themselves some more roast.

Bokka, however, was a little way off, leaning back against a hazel bush which looked like it had been left when the fields were cleared. It had several parallel trunks and she'd chosen the closest to the fire, but it still wasn't very close. She couldn't serve herself more food—and maybe she didn't want to; she'd emptied a bowl and put it down by her side. She also couldn't easily join in with the conversation, although looking at the distance, Laki thought she could probably hear it.

"She's always like that," Pru said. Startled, Laki jerked her head back to focus on the young woman sitting next to her. "Doesn't sit with us, I mean. Doesn't join in with things. Doesn't behave like a normal person."

Laki shrugged. She didn't like Pru talking that way, but she was a guest in a new village. She'd only met Pru that afternoon. What did she know? Instead of pursuing that line of conversation, or trying to bring it back to the tomb–building question, she asked something she thought Heln should have brought up sooner. "When are your trading days?"

"Trading days?"

"Yes, you know, the days when you come together, maybe with another village or two, and trading is allowed?"

Pru frowned. "We don't have anything like that. Why wouldn't you be allowed to trade every day?"

Laki didn't know. Things were obviously very different here and perhaps—if they didn't have to wait but could trade immediately—this visit might not be very long.

*

Most of the newcomers were not interesting. Bokka had sussed them out as they met others from Cow Village on the beach; there was an older man and two younger people who seemed very interested in what Genu had to say.

One of them was different. The youngest, a young woman, was not so interested in Genu and tombs and those things. She had a necklace which Bokka would have liked to touch and a round, smiling face which seemed friendly. Pru kept talking to her, but Pru was not interesting and Bokka thought that the young woman who had recently arrived could be convinced to talk to someone else instead.

Someone like Bokka.

Maybe more than talk.

She didn't let herself fully form that thought. She didn't get many chances to meet new people, and she wanted to do better this time.

The hazel tree she was leaning against was comfortable. Standing up and going to speak to someone would be difficult. Bokka challenged herself: if you talk to her, if she answers you, you are allowed to go and work on polishing your stone ball.

Slowly, she stood up. Trying to be casual, she ambled towards the group. The oldest new arrival—Sal?—was telling a story about a mistake that had been made in a building project – probably a tomb?—where a big stone had slipped and fallen on someone's foot. The injury had been minor, and the way he told it made the others laugh. Bokka thought it sounded painful.

Bokka was about to speak when Pru looked up and scowled. "What do you want?"

She must have approached them in the wrong way somehow. Avoiding the temptation to turn back to the hazel tree and pretend this hadn't happened, Bokka said, "I only wanted some more meat."

Pru waved a magnanimous hand towards the fire, as if it were hers to give away, rather than hunted by a whole group and butchered by Storna and Aiso and prepared for cooking by Aiso's son and generally the product of much work by many people. Bokka ignored her and stepped forward, taking her little flint blade from her leather tool belt to cut away a fine slice of meat. It wasn't much, no more than a taste; she wasn't really hungry. She rolled it in her fingers and ate it. At least while she was chewing she had an excuse to look and not talk.

There was more chatter, Genu telling another allegedly amusing injury story, but Bokka ignored them. When she'd swallowed the meat she was chewing, she said to the newly arrived young woman, "What's your name?"

"Laki."

"I like your necklace." It was a good necklace; Bokka could tell at once that it had been made from many different materials, from the bones and teeth of different animals, even some she couldn't immediately recognise.

"Thank you, I made it myself." Laki's fingers were long and scarred with the marks of carving tools, but they stroked the two tusk pendants on the necklace gently.

"Did it take you a long time?"

Laki paused over that, head tilted. "Sort of. I worked in stages. I did the little beads first."

"Cow's teeth and sheep bone?" Bokka tried to make it sound like a question, although she knew.

14

"That's right." Laki didn't sound upset about Bokka already knowing that. In fact, when Bokka glanced up from the necklace to Laki's mouth, she was smiling. "And several of the bigger ones are from a whale's teeth. This massive whale was washed ashore near our village last year and we made all sorts of things from it."

"We get whales sometimes," Bokka agreed.

She was about to tell Laki about the one which had beached itself, alive, and what it had sounded like, and what it has smelled like, when Pru cut in. "I'm sure you brought lots of beautiful things with you to trade."

"We did." Laki knew that she was there to trade and as she started to tell Pru about all the things they had brought, she knew she should have been glad for the chance—but she wasn't. She regretted not being able to hear what Bokka had to say about whales.

Chapter 2

AS THE SUN SET, PEOPLE DRIFTED away from the fire and towards bed. Marko and Sal happily went with hosts who could find spare sleeping spaces here or there, but Laki hung back—she'd been offered a bed in Genu and Pru's house, but she didn't feel keen to take it up—and managed to speak to Heln alone as they strolled together towards the village.

"How long are we staying if they don't have trading days?"

Heln shrugged. "As long as it takes to do the trading we need to do." Ey must have heard Laki's sigh, because ey added softly, "It can help us, you know. We can leave at any time, so we can say we'll go and take our goods with us. It encourages them to agree to our suggested trades."

Laki hadn't thought of it like that. "But will we really go?"

"Yes, when we're ready. You know the plan is to find at least one or two more places to trade before we start back to Otter Village for the winter."

"How will you know when we're ready?"

"I'll look at what we've traded and what we've got in return, what we've got left, the weather, what we're told about other villages around here..." Heln glanced at Laki sideways and slowed eir pace even further. "And I'll listen to what my crew tell me. If you want to go, or if you want to stay, I'll take that into account. Is there something I need to know?"

Laki kept herself moving, although her first instinct was to stop and think about it. "Not really. I don't know. Some of the people here..."

"You need to give yourself some time," Heln told her gently. "When I first travelled with my aunt, she used to say it took three nights in a new village to get used to the local standards."

"And sometimes after three nights you had to leave in a hurry." Laki had heard the stories.

"Sometimes we had to leave," Heln agreed, and she could tell from the tension in eir voice that ey was also thinking of those stories. "My point is that you should give yourself three nights to get to know the place and the people. Don't judge them too soon; when you see them in the morning as well as the evening, it'll help you to see what's the crop and what's weed."

"I'd better go," Laki said, gesturing to where Pru was waiting at the entrance to the underground part of the village, scallop shell lamp in hand.

"Sleep well." Heln gave her a quick hug. "And tell me tomorrow if there is something I need to know."

"I will." With another sigh, not sure what she was sad about, Laki went to follow Pru into the village.

*

"Goodnight!" Marko called as he met Heln at the door of another house. Laki was left alone with Genu and Pru.

At the door, she paused, letting her eyes adjust to the relative darkness. There was a fire in the hearth which had burned down low and stone shelves with nicely decorated cooking pots and eating bowls almost exactly like the ones at home. There were four stone box beds, two obviously well used with ruffled furs and spare clothes hung around them. Pru immediately crossed to one of the unused ones, shaking out some of the furs which were piled there and reaching into the base, presumably to check that it was comfortable, or that nothing which shouldn't be in a bed at all had been hidden among the covers.

Genu didn't fuss with anything. He didn't talk, or even look at Pru or Laki. He re–tied his hair in a looser style, dropped the clothes he'd been wearing on the floor, and slid naked between the furs on his bed. Before Pru stood up from the bed she was preparing for Laki, Genu was snoring.

"Make yourself comfortable," Pru said. "Leave the fire alone, we don't stoke it up until the morning. There's water in that bowl if you want some—for drinking. We'll fetch more for washing in the morning. Don't worry if you hear strange noises in the night. It's probably my dad—you can hear him already."

"Oh." Laki put her bag down on the bed and began to untie the thongs. "Thank you."

"If you need anything else, please try and wait until the morning. I'm tired."

"Yes, of course," Laki said, imagining that she would simply sneak out of the house as soon as Pru was asleep. "I'm sure I'll be fine, thank you." She made a show of combing her hair and picking her teeth with a small stick. Fortunately, Pru turned away and didn't try to watch her undress. Despite her ideas about sneaking away, the day of rowing and meeting new people and exploring Cow Village caught up with her. As soon as she curled up in the furs with the smooth beads of her necklace in her hands, she fell asleep while she could still hear Pru moving around, tidying something.

When she woke, she couldn't be sure whether it was morning or not. At home, a little daylight would creep in at the doorway, even if the rest of the house had been carefully sealed against winter winds. Here, the front door only opened onto an underground passage, and the only light was the vague red glow from the embers in the hearth. It wasn't enough to see by, only enough to know that she had opened her eyes.

For a while she lay there, worrying about the day ahead and struggling to picture what would happen. What did they even eat for breakfast here?

She didn't feel like she'd slept, but she opened her eyes again a while later to find the house distinctly brighter. Pru was kneeling at the hearth, blowing on the embers and adding small sticks to bring the fire back to life. Overhead, a single sunbeam crept in through a gap between the top of the stone wall and the turf roof. *If I'd known there was a gap,* Laki thought, *I would have known that it wasn't dawn yet.*

She stayed still and watched Pru work. Once the fire was going well, she took a scrap of leather off the top of a pottery bowl and divided the sourdough mix inside. She added some flour to one part and put it back under the cover while she mixed the rest into a dough and left it to rise for later. She moved some things around on the shelves—perhaps she was getting wheat ready to grind, or something. Laki couldn't really see, especially as Pru's back was to her.

Suddenly Genu lurched upright. "I'm hungry."

Shocked, Laki was glad that she'd decided to stay still and pretend to be asleep for a bit longer.

Pru clattered a pot. "Not long now, I just got the fire going."

"Only just?"

"Well, not long ago, and I had to..."

"Never mind all that. Your old dad needs food."

"I'm going as fast as I can," Pru said. She stirred something, poured water from a bowl, and scraped a couple of hot stones from the embers so that she could drop them into a cooking bag. Steam rose at once and with it came the smell of sheep's meat cooking.

*

A few walls away, Nerto was bustling about eir hearth and making a similar breakfast: meat from a sheep butchered a few days ago, reheated in a thick gravy, with some marsh samphire from the shoreline. Ey swished the seawater in the storage box, checking whether the limpets Bokka had collected yesterday were still alive, and put the day's portion of wheat ready for Klamro to make into flour later.

As ey worked, ey listened to Bokka explaining the polishing process she was using on a stone axe-head she was finishing. "At the end I might even use a pad of wool and some sand from the beach to see if I can get it to really shine."

"That sounds good," Nerto said without looking up. The door opened and Klamro came back, carrying a big jar of fresh water from the spring. "Ah, excellent."

Klamro nodded as ey passed it over. Soon, all three of them were settled around the fire with their food.

"What are you doing today?" Nerto asked.

Bokka's mouth was full but she held up the half–polished axe as illustration.

"And we'll probably spend some time with the visitors," Klamro said. "They said they've come to trade and pointed at their bags of things, but there are bound to be stories and ideas as well."

"Agree." Nerto chewed thoughtfully. "I hope we can learn from them."

Bokka thought about the young woman she had spoken to the night before who had replied and not turned away and who had been willing to talk about that beautiful necklace. Her parents' idea sounded good to her.

*

By the time they settled down to eat, with the sun casting long shadows, Laki felt that she was getting the hang of the trading thing. She had spent the morning helping with—and mainly admiring—the cows, whose big eyes and gentle noses had investigated her thoroughly. They weren't planning to trade for animals, but Marko had taken an interest in one of the young bulls.

"We weren't sure whether to keep him," Nerto had explained. "More than we need for the herd, really, but he's..." Ey waved a hand to indicate the bull's size, colour, personality, and more. Looking at him, and his equally handsome age mates, Laki could understand that the village had struggled to choose which of the males to slaughter and which to keep.

Once the cows were grazing happily around the trees, they'd left them with a couple of the children as guards and moved on to a tour of the fields. There were the usual patches of wheat and beans. Not far into the forest, there was a space which had been cleared and then abandoned.

"It's where Genu wants to build the tomb." Nerto shrugged. Heln took the chance to ask more. "We were hearing a lot about that last night. Are you very close to starting work? We were only planning a short visit, but if you need the extra pairs of hands..."

Nerto shrugged again, eir shoulders coming almost to touch eir ears as ey suggested eir doubt. "Genu's been talking about it all winter. I don't know. We've always taken our dead to the water, or a few of my family wanted to go the old way, into the top of a tree for the eagles. I'm not sure what a tomb is for. I mean, it sounds very small. Genu says only good people are allowed into the tomb and it means you get more help from your ancestors, because you've kept them close, but there's room for everyone in the sea, and it's not like we're ever far away from them."

"I'm glad we have a tomb in Otter Village," Marko said. "That doesn't mean you should build one, of course. But when my grandfather was murdered, he was put into our tomb, and when the man who killed him died, he was put into the sea, so they don't have to be together."

"But aren't some of your other ancestors in the sea?" Nerto had tipped eir head to the side, considering.

"They are," Marko said, and went on to retell a story Trebbi had told him, about ancestors in the sea getting mixed up together like the sand on the ocean floor. It was a good story, but Laki had heard it before.

When Pru said, "It's such a lovely warm evening, let's go for a swim," several people agreed.

"I'll go with them," Laki said aside to Heln, not disturbing Marko's story, and Heln gave her a twinkling smile and a quick nod.

*

Genu called Bokka back as she was about to follow the group to the water. "Don't you start bothering my daughter again," he said. "Stay here. You ought to be learning about trading, anyway; you're always making those polished toys and you ought to know what they're worth."

They were worth about the same as a polished axe-head which took the same amount of time to make, and Bokka knew that perfectly well from previous trading visits to local villages. She wondered whether Genu had forgotten about those or whether he was making an excuse to keep her with the older group who were staying on the shore.

"They're not only toys," she said reflexively. "Some of the villages give decorated stone balls like the ones I make to the ancestors, you know. You should be encouraging me to make lots so you can put them in your tomb."

"Our ancestors don't want that kind of silly thing," Genu told her with a sneer. "It's a waste of your skills when you could be making something useful."

Marko had finished his story and Sal said something which made Heln and Nerto laugh, and Marko choke on his food. It distracted Genu from talking to Bokka. Heln pounded Marko on the back.

While Genu wasn't looking, Bokka got up and walked away. She didn't want to talk to Pru anyway. The old man needn't worry about her bothering his daughter. Not that she ever really bothered Pru, or at least no more than Pru bothered her. What did he know? She didn't really want to swim, either. Stripping off, leaping into the water... despite the warm evening air, she knew the water would be cold.

Those who had gone in were keeping themselves warm with vigorous swimming. Pru started a game by using her cupped hands to splash water into Laki's face. Laki gave as good as she got, dousing Pru with water from behind and eliciting a shriek, and the swimming descended into a chaotic water fight.

Just as well I'm not out there, Bokka told herself. *I'd be confused. I wouldn't like it.* Despite that, she still wanted to be near them, and she went and sat by the piles of clothes which had been left on the beach, picking up some seashells from the high tide line so that she could say to anyone who asked—and herself—that she was searching for the brightly coloured swirls.

As she searched along, something else caught her eye. On Laki's pile of clothes, half–hidden in the folds of her leather tunic, the gleam of polished bone... Bokka picked up Laki's necklace. For a moment she held it as she had held the little spiral seashells. Then, with her back to the gathering around the cooking fire and ignored by the swimmers, she tucked it into the pouch at her belt. She carried on working her way slowly along the tideline, away from the piles of clothes.

She found a stone the greyish–green of heather, and one with bright white lines running through it, and one which was the perfect shape for a hammer. She tucked some stones and shells in her pouch on top of the necklace, which was lovely and smooth and had been near Laki's skin. And everyone else had seen it there, so they didn't need to know that Bokka had it now.

From the beach, she took the long way back to the village, winding around the far side to avoid walking right past the cooking fire and the people there. She hoped neither of her parents would be home.

She was out of luck on that one. Klamro looked up as she came in and smiled. "Have you had a good day?" Ey hadn't been at the communal meal, she realised. She should have gone up to the top of the cliff or into the woods where she could be alone, but if she left now, ey would ask why and she wouldn't be able to lie about the necklace in her pouch.

"Adequate," she said. She sat down next to em and joined in with the task ey'd started—teasing out the handfuls of wool they had collected from the sheep and rolling it, between the hands or down the thigh, into yarn.

There wasn't enough from their little flock of sheep who shed wool in the spring to do much with it, but rolled into short lengths of yarn it was useful for tying up bundles and threading jewellery. She hadn't noticed whether Laki's necklace was strung on wool or leather or nettle string or something else. She wanted to get it out and have a good look, but she didn't want Klamro to be angry with her. Not that she'd done anything wrong, she hurried to assure herself. It was only that ey would ask questions, and ey might recognise it as Laki's, and ey might say she should return it now. She didn't need to hear that because she'd give it back soon anyway. When she'd had a good look.

"What do you think of these traders, then?"

The question startled Bokka out of her thoughts and she froze, hands midway through rolling the yarn up her thigh. "Err... which one?"

"Any," Klamro said. "They all seem to know each other fairly well."

"They're all from the same village."

"Well, they are all living in Otter Village now," Klamro said. Eir fingers were busy teasing out little bundles of wool, but when Bokka glanced up at eir face, ey was gazing into the fire as if it were in the far distance. "But I think Heln came from somewhere else originally."

"Ey has a different way of speaking," Bokka agreed. She'd noticed the way ey pronounced Marko's name, which made it sound soft and warm, not as hard as the way Laki said it. She hadn't heard Laki say her own name. Sal had mentioned her once or twice. She hadn't really noticed how he'd pronounced it. She should have been paying more attention.

She should have been paying more attention, because Klamro had said something and she'd missed it. She shook her head and ey repeated, "Sal was telling us about the house he built. He seems like a skilled man."

"Laki is skilled, too," Bokka agreed.

"Oh yes? What does she make?"

Oops. Bokka hadn't meant to talk about the necklace, so she shook her head and asked, "Did any of them talk to you about the sheep yet?"

*

They played in the shallow water for a while, not really swimming but alternating between splashing water over each other and sitting in the surf talking. Laki was getting a bit tired of Pru's attitude, and the opportunity to douse her with sea water—it's just a game!—when she got too annoying was refreshing. She also enjoyed getting to know Pru's friend Storna a bit better. Storna was more mature than Pru and had set up a household of her own until her partner had died suddenly of a fever. Now Storna was living with her parents again but looking for a new partner.

Laki tried her best to answer questions about the others in the group. Marko and Heln are already partners, so there's no more to say. Sal? Well, Sal's a good man. He's always lived in Otter Village although his mother was from Dog Village. He's strong and good at big tasks—good at felling a tree or lifting stones for a house.

"Or a tomb?" Storna asked.

"He helped build ours," Laki agreed. "I'm too young to really remember it, but he talks about it sometimes."

"How old is he, then? I didn't think he was that much older than you."

"Oh, yes, he must be... eight or ten summers older than me?"

"And he's not partnered? Why is that?"

Laki could only shrug. She'd known Sal a little bit all her life and had got to know him much better on their journey round the islands. His not having a partner was simply a fact about the world, not something to ask questions about.

"And how old are you now?" Pru asked.

"This will be my twentieth summer."

"Oh, you were born in the weird year, same as Bokka," Pru said before Laki could ask how old she was. A bigger wave than usual rolled in, and Storna dumped two cupped handfuls of water over Pru's head, and Pru shrieked and splashed back.

"Enough," Storna said, and walked out of the water. Laki followed, and after a moment Pru came, too, grumbling.

They took their time strolling back to their clothes, drying their skin in the cool evening air, and shivering a bit. Pru and Storna started a conversation about building houses which relied on knowledge of Cow Village Laki didn't really have. She let it pass her by.

When she picked up her tunic, she thought at once that something was missing, but it wasn't until she'd pulled on her leggings as well that she was sure.

"Where's my necklace?" she asked, turning to look at the beach around her. Maybe it had simply been moved away from where she left it. There were plenty of shells and stones and bone—coloured things which could disguise it if it were sitting on the sand somewhere nearby.

"I haven't seen it," Pru said at once. Laki pictured her, jealous, sneaking back to the clothes and stealing it, hiding it. Ridiculous, of course—there hadn't been a chance, hadn't been a moment when they weren't in sight of each other. But she'd answered so quickly, almost defensively...

"We'll look," Storna said. "Where did you leave it?"

"Here, with my clothes. It was on top of my tunic, and then I folded the tunic over a bit so the necklace was out of sight."

"And you're sure it's gone?"

"It wasn't in my tunic, or my leggings, or my shoes," Laki said, waving a hand at her body to demonstrate that she was now wearing all these items and had checked them thoroughly.

"You didn't put it in one of your pouches?" Storna asked, looking at Laki's belt, still on the beach.

"I don't think so." But Laki checked anyway, opening each of her three pouches in turn. Dried tinder fungus in case she needed kindling. A small hammer stone she especially liked and a piece of antler just the right shape for knapping a flint precisely. Water mint she'd found in a stream earlier in the day and was saving to chew at bedtime. No bone and tooth beads, no necklace.

While she was doing that, Storna had started searching the sand, kneeling down and running her hands over the area where Laki's clothes had been. She turned over several stones which were the same colours, and was briefly distracted by a pretty yellow periwinkle shell, but found no sign of the necklace on the ground.

"I'm sure I left it here." Laki felt her fingers shaking as she closed the pouches again. It couldn't have gone far. She'd spent so long working on it.

"You didn't wear it into the water," Pru assured her, "and you were wearing it earlier in the day, so you must have left it here, really."

"So where is it?" Laki tried to keep her voice even, but she was on the verge of tears, and she knew other people could tell because Heln and Marko were standing up from around the fire.

Heln reached her first and put a comforting arm around her shoulders. "What's the matter?"

Laki explained. Marko searched the beach again.

"Is there anywhere else it could be?" Heln asked. "You checked your clothes, your pouches... could you have left it inside Pru's house?"

"No, I was wearing it by the fire earlier."

The sun was setting and Storna said, "We've looked for it here. It's not on the beach, or if it is, we can't see it and we're not going to tonight."

"Could someone else have taken it?" Heln asked. "Several people have gone back to the village, and some of them walked past the piles of clothes while you were swimming."

Laki looked around and saw that it was true: Sal had gone, and Genu and Bokka and a few others.

"Nobody in our village would do that!" Pru said hotly.

Heln shrugged. "Perhaps it's a misunderstanding. Someone could have thought they were being helpful."

"Maybe a bird flew off with it," Pru suggested, still sounding grumpy.

"We can check the nests tomorrow," Storna agreed, "and have eggs to eat as well."

"The eagles on the..."

"It's my necklace," Laki said, interrupting Pru. People were trying to help but the conversation seemed to be losing focus; it was her necklace which was missing, and her feelings which were hurt, and it should be her decision about what happened next. Or at least have some say in it. "It's too heavy for a bird to carry. Everyone saw me wearing it, so if they picked it up, they knew it was mine. Maybe Sal was worried about it getting lost and took it into the village for me." That didn't seem likely, either, but at least it opened a positive possibility.

"Let's go in." Heln let eir arm drop from Laki's shoulders and the group moved slowly towards the village. "Laki, do you want to check in Pru's house first in case someone left it there for you?"

"Good idea," Laki said, glad that Heln was picking up on her preferences. "And in the morning we'll look out here again, and ask everyone, and it'll probably turn up somewhere."

Chapter 3

EVENTUALLY KLAMRO AND NERTO WERE CURLED into their beds, and Bokka thought they must be asleep. Very gently, very quietly, she slipped the necklace out from the place where she'd hidden it. She'd heard the echoes of conversation along the alley and she knew Laki had missed it. When she'd picked it up, she'd wanted to touch it and especially to admire the shine on the curves of the two tusk pendants. Now, holding it, she also enjoyed the sense of power it gave her. For once, she had something that someone else wanted.

She could use this to get Laki's attention. If she gave it back in the morning... no. If she handed it back, Laki would know that she had taken it, and Laki would be angry, not glad. If she said that she had found it, perhaps if she went to the beach as soon as the sun rose and said she had found it there... would Laki guess what had really happened? She might. Bokka didn't want to take that risk. And anyway, that would soon be over. It would be one conversation, one handing back of the necklace, and Laki might never speak to her again.

Better idea: she would offer to help search. They would go over the whole village together, and the beach, and the path, and they would talk and laugh while they were searching. Then, eventually, they would find the necklace—Bokka would find the necklace—in the last place they'd thought to look, and Laki would be so pleased, and she'd smile and hug Bokka, and Bokka would hug her back and their bodies would be pressed together and Laki's breasts would be warm against hers and...

In the midst of this enjoyable plan, Bokka drifted off to sleep, the necklace tangled in her fingers.

*

The waves, which had been a pleasant place to play in the evening, haunted Laki's fitful sleep. The tide would climb the beach, towards the place where her clothes had been left. It would probably only reach to the line of dry seaweed—the mark of the water's further extent—but sometimes a stray wave could go further. And if her necklace had been dropped below that line, it would be gone.

Waking to find everything dark, Laki wondered whether enough of her own ancestors had gone into the sea that someone down there would be willing to try and help her. Her mother was in the tomb in Otter Village, as were her mother's parents, but some before that—because there had to be a time before the tomb was built—would have been placed in the sea. She imagined an ancestor–spirit, perhaps in the form of a seal or a walrus, finding her necklace on the sea floor. Would they recognise it as something important? Would they recognise it as something made in part from their own kind? Would they recognise it as human work to be returned to the shore?

She rolled over and tried to settle herself more comfortably in the bed. On the other side of the house, Genu snored. He had been disinterested to the point of dismissiveness when they got back and told him what had happened; everyone else had at least asked questions about where they had looked, but Genu had only said, "Weird" and asked Pru about what food there would be to eat in the morning.

Not useful. Laki realised she'd assumed that, as the village leader, Genu would take a central role in looking for her necklace—would help her ask people to look round their homes, would release people from their ordinary work to help with the search. It seemed like that wouldn't happen at all. She wished he was nicer. She wished he would stop snoring. She wished she hadn't gone swimming.

Sadness rose in the back of her throat, threatening to choke her. She wished she was at home, even though the house was horribly empty without her mother; she wished she'd never come trading at all. She hadn't meant to give her necklace away. She hadn't even meant to trade it and to get nothing in return... She forced herself to breathe slowly, avoiding noisy sobs, and wiped her eyes with the back of her hand.

She tried to think of other things instead. All the talk about tombs here made it hard to avoid thinking about the one at home. Instead of remembering the funeral, and her mother's body being taken inside, and the story she overheard—almost certainly not meant for her ears, but impossible to stop listening to when it was told within earshot—about the way bones inside the tomb had to be moved to make space for new arrivals. She tried to remember what it was like to stand by the tomb later, when the moon had emptied and filled a couple of times, but she still missed her mother every day.

The tomb was near the sea, at the top of the cliffs. There was a grassy area around the tomb itself where people came fairly often, bringing sheep and cows past or walking from one set of fields to another. There were trees on the inland side, mainly hazel and elm. The hazels were densely packed and surrounded by herbs and shrubs in places, although one stood almost alone because it was the place the cows had chosen to rub their itches and trampled down all the smaller plants around it. The sea crashed on the rocks below. It wasn't a spot with a beach. But from the top of the cliff, you could see some distance, and it had been another day about that time when Trebbi came back to the village and told them that a whale had beached.

And Laki had used a tooth from the whale to make beads, and she'd used the beads to make a necklace, and the necklace might now be in the sea again.

She could hear the waves. In the morning she would search. Somewhere in these knotted thoughts Laki must have fallen asleep again, because she woke with a jump to the sound of Pru putting a big pottery bowl down on something stone. Sunlight came in through the little gap. The firelight was high. She could smell food. *It must be morning.*

Somehow, she'd thought she was lying on the beach itself because she could hear the waves so clearly. It took her a while to work out where she was, and how to move her limbs, and decide that it was probably best to sit up and see if there was something to eat.

As soon as she did, Pru handed her a bowl of porridge and a wooden spoon. Genu had already gone out.

"A sheep escaped in the night and they've gone to try and find it," Pru explained. "Don't you worry, it doesn't usually take long. There's a panic and then the sheep comes back when it gets lonely."

"Okay." Laki applied herself to her food instead of asking questions. It turned out she didn't need to ask; Pru answered them anyway.

"And don't worry about searching for your necklace without Genu, I'll help you. I'm the leader's daughter and we'll go round and ask to look in people's houses. It'll mostly be kids at home anyway, with everyone else out looking for this sheep, so there won't be any trouble. Someone must have stolen it, but I know all the good hiding places in these houses and we'll find it soon."

*

Something had woken her. The necklace was still in her hands—in front of her face, above the furs which covered her body, in full view of anyone who walked past her bed. Bokka immediately moved to hide it. Then she realised that she didn't know who else was in the house. She had spoken to Klamro last night, but had her other parent come in at some point? Panic gripped her. If Nerto had come in, had she seen the necklace? Was it visible in the firelight?

Then she realised that the thing which had woken her was a noise. Someone was at the door. That was actually a reason to panic, because it was very unusual to have a visitor in the early morning.

In case someone was watching, she made a show of stretching and yawning, using the movement to push the stolen necklace further down into her bed. Then she got up and went to the door. She was naked, so she didn't open it far; only enough to peep round the edge and see who was there.

"Sheep missing," said Aiso, which was a full explanation.

"Coming," Bokka said. "I'll wake my parents."

Aiso nodded his thanks, already moving on to the next door.

"Sheep missing," Bokka repeated, shaking Nerto's shoulder. On the other side of the house, Klamro was stirring anyway. Nerto was the deeper sleeper, and Klamro wouldn't take much waking.

"Go away," Nerto managed to say before burrowing deeper into eir furs.

"I can't," Bokka said. "Everyone will be wanted, there's a sheep missing."

"It's okay," Klamro said. Ey had climbed out of eir bed and was throwing on clothes. "You get dressed, Bokka. We'll go and Nerto will follow us soon."

Get dressed. Bokka pulled her leggings and tunic on but then paused. She really wanted to put the necklace in her pouch and take it with her; if she left it here, it might be found by Nerto tidying up the house if nobody else. But if she stopped to fill her pouches, Klamro would wonder what was taking her so long. And if she was out looking for a sheep all day, how would she hide the necklace somewhere in the village and lead Laki to it?

Next to her, Nerto had sat up and Klamro had come over to give em a kiss. "Come and join us as soon as you can," ey said.

They could both see Bokka, and the sides of the bed would hardly hide her hands. She left the necklace where it was.

*

Pru and Laki took their time getting ready. The first door they were about to try opened before they could even knock, and Nerto came out. "All off to help find this sheep?" ey asked.

"My father says we aren't all needed," Pru said. It sounded so lazy that Laki couldn't help making a face, and when she looked at Nerto, she could see that they were in agreement. "We're looking for Laki's necklace!" Pru added defensively.

"I'm sure that will wait," Nerto said. "The sheep might be dying somewhere or getting further and further away from the village. The necklace will stay wherever it's been left."

Laki wanted her necklace back, but she didn't want to search for it alone with Pru, and she saw Nerto's point. She sighed deeply, demonstratively. "Ey's right, Pru," she said. She made an exaggerated sad face. "My necklace will have to wait. We need to go and help with the sheep."
"My father said I didn't!" Pru's voice echoed off the stone walls and roof of the narrow alley between houses.

Nerto and Laki simply watched her as she listened and heard herself for once.

"If he sends me back, it was your fault," she muttered.

"You could stay and make sure nothing else happens here," Nerto said gently. "Laki and I will go. You keep a watch and be here to explain to anyone else—someone might still be asleep."

"I expect Chok stayed behind with her new baby. I could go and sit with them."

*

It was a mild day, grey with a very light drizzle which hung drops of water on the tight curls of Laki's hair. She watched one of the dogs bound through a stream and shake itself enthusiastically, and she thought that maybe she should do the same. Before she went back into the village, at least, so that as much of the water as possible stayed outside.

Having no idea where to look for any sheep, or how to tell which one was the missing one if she saw it, she simply followed Storna up to a huddle of people with Genu at the centre.

"Guests don't need to help," Genu said as soon as he saw her.

"But I'm happy to," Laki replied. She might have preferred to be indoors, or searching for her necklace, but she didn't want to be put down and left out of what was clearly a major event for the community.

Genu couldn't really stop her, so he ignored her. He was sharing out tasks, asking pairs of people to go in different directions and look in different places—these people to check the fields, those to go down to the lake, others to go to the shore and the cliffs. He assigned Storna to go with an older woman, Amros. He didn't give Laki anything to do. She followed Storna, though, and nobody objected.

As they walked out to the area of woods where Genu had asked them to search, Amros introduced herself and they discovered that she'd met Laki's mother, Smeka, many years ago.

"It's the highlight of any child's year, to go to the party at the great standing stones. I remember meeting several people from Otter Village. Smeka was so much fun, too. We snuck away with a bowl of beer which was meant to be shared with twenty people, and there were only four of us, and we got absolutely roaring drunk."

"She did like to have a beer," Laki agreed. "Right up until she died that was one of the things she enjoyed."

"Did she have a good life?" Amros asked as they reached the edge of the field and slowed down, following a track between the trees and making a point of looking all around.

Laki wasn't sure how to answer that. "She did her best," she said eventually. "She suffered a lot with toothache and problems in her mouth. She could be... grumpy."

"I can imagine." Amros stopped on the path in front of Laki. Storna was behind them and almost bumped into her.

Amros held up a hand, signalling for silence, then pointed forward. Between the trees there was a little flash of white.

"Is it?" Storna hissed.

Amros shrugged. "Dunno," she said softly. "Got to try."

Storna leaned forward and made a pinching gesture with her hand, widely spread fingers coming together. Amros nodded. She pointed to herself and forward down the path which would take her to in front of the sheep, then to Laki and the ground she was standing on, then slightly forward. Storna pointed her own way through the bushes to the back of the sheep.

If it worked, it would be neat and they would trap it easily. Laki edged forward slowly as the other two set off to their positions. The edges of the path had been grazed by various animals being brought along, and trodden down by people walking past, but after a few steps she was into taller plants. She managed to go around a small clump of stinging nettles. She was checking that she could still see the sheep, and working out a route to get closer, when there was a sharp snapping sound to her left. Storna had broken a twig.

The sheep's head jerked up. For a moment, Laki thought it was going to stay there.

It bolted. They ran after it. Laki managed to stay close enough to see it run almost into the arms of Klamro, who had appeared on another path through the trees. Klamro didn't try and catch the sheep bodily. Ey let it run past, then produced a handful of sweet herbs from behind eir back and made a clicking noise with eir tongue.

The sheep swerved. There was recognition, Laki thought, slowing her steps so as not to startle it again. It took a mouthful from Klamro's hand as Bokka came up behind it and took a firm hold on the wool at the back of its neck.

"Good work," Klamro said to her. Ey unlooped a rope from eir belt and put a collar on the sheep. In that instant, Laki felt herself relax—the problem was solved, at least for now.

"Well done," Laki said to them both, stepping onto the path. They hadn't seen her approach, and Bokka visibly startled with a jerk.

"Sorry for scaring it." Storna came out of the bushes with Amros close behind.

Klamro shrugged. "Easily done. She wouldn't come to most people like that, but I raised her when she was a lamb and so she knows me."

Bokka took the rope from em. "Better get her back to Genu before he sends anyone else out searching."

*

Bokka kept her hands and her eyes occupied with the sheep. It would be silly to let her run away again now that they had got her. And if Bokka was obviously, visibly busy, it stopped anyone else trying to talk to her. She hadn't wanted to come out, and now she wanted to get back to the house—back to the necklace and the need to hide it where it could be "found" later—as soon as possible.

This was not to be, of course. When she delivered the sheep to Genu, he was pleased. Klamro had to step in to tell the whole story, with comments from Storna about her mistake and from Amros about how the spot of white had appeared through the trees and from Laki about how she'd not known what to do because she didn't know the woods... Then the sheep had to be counted to check. Then everyone else had to be fetched back. Bokka found herself running down to the beach to call to people.

When she got there, she hardly had breath or words to explain. Aiso asked, "Has it been found?" and all she could do was nod.

Back in the village, everyone was standing around chatting. They were sharing food, whatever was left from the night before. Everyone was hungry, and Pru and Chok had played with the baby rather than cooking. They swapped stories and wondered what to do next. Some of the normal things would need doing, and some extra people would be needed to help make sure no more sheep got separated from the flock, and there were traders visiting, and what about the fields?

Bokka squeezed through the crowds along the corridor. When she got to her house, she found it blessedly empty. She had seen Nerto already grinding flour for the day, and Klamro was probably still with the sheep.

She started the day again. She got back into bed, wrapping the necklace around her fingers—this time making sure to keep it under the cover of one of her softest furs. It wasn't quiet, with the echoes of conversation coming in from outside, but with the fire down to embers and the walls and roof carefully plugged against the winter storms, it was almost dark. She made a new plan. She would wait for everyone to go out to their work. She would say she was tired and would come soon. And when she was alone in the village, she would go and hide the necklace.

It was a good plan. It was a good necklace. She stroked one of the curved tusks which hung down—at the front as Laki usually wore it, at the front where it touched the soft brown skin of Laki's chest and the place where her breast began to fill out—and enjoyed the smooth polish it had been given. She wanted her decorated stone ball to feel like that when she was finished with it. It was true that she was tired. The furs warmed up around her and she dozed off to sleep.

*

With the lost sheep back in the herd, what had been an organised search process descended into chaos, or at least it seemed like that to Laki. Genu had a knot of people around him telling and retelling the way the sheep was found. Others disappeared into the village, or went out to the fields, or down to the beach. She tried to tell herself that it was okay, they had their own things to do, but it was a disappointment after a brief vision of a proper, organised search for her necklace.

Heln must have noticed her looking glum, because ey and Marko came over. When ey put eir arm around her shoulders, tears started in her eyes, and ey said, "We're going to search, Laki, you'll see."

Genu didn't seem so sure. When Heln put it to him, he said, "Necklaces aren't as important as living sheep."

"It's still important to us." Heln replied.

Genu turned an assessing gaze on Laki, lingering on the bare brown skin at her neck before resting on her breasts. She'd added a few cow–tooth beads to the soft leather of her tunic but she didn't think that was what had drawn his attention.

"Maybe some of the others will help you," he said, shrugging as if that was a major concession. "Don't take them away from their usual work, but if they've got time to help, so be it. Try my daughter. She's normally not doing anything useful."

"I don't like the way they talk about each other here," Heln muttered into Marko's ear, just loud enough for Laki to pick it up as well, as they walked back to the village.

"They're not all as bad as that," Marko replied, equally softly. "But I know what you mean."

As they entered the covered alley which formed the centre of the village, Pru's head appeared round one of the doors – not her own home, but probably Storna's, Laki guessed. "Ah, there you are," she said. "I got bored waiting for everyone to come back, and Chok's no fun when the baby's asleep, so I started searching for your necklace."

That was so helpful and thoughtful, Laki knew she should be grateful, although it also seemed a little like stepping on Laki's toes. "Thank you," she said anyway. "Have you found anything?"

"No, but I've only done two houses." Pru indicated the one she was in, and the one next to it. "I started with houses because I'm here, but you could also go down to the beach again. And check along the paths we walked in case it was dropped somewhere."

Laki could have thought of those things herself. She almost growled. "Thank you for your help," she said again, as much to remind herself that Pru was, in fact, trying to help, and not trying to take away the search for the necklace which had already been lost. "I thought we should check at the hearth, too, in case the cord broke while we were eating and I didn't notice."

"I could go and do that," Heln offered. "I need to meet someone who's interested in trading for some of our stone axes. We'll want to test them on the trees Genu needs cutting down, and I think they're somewhere over that way."

Laki nodded and looked around. More people were returning from the search for the lost sheep. Some walked past, or entered the village from the other end of the alley, and went straight into their houses. A few were hanging around, listening. She recognised Storna and Bokka and a few other faces to which she couldn't yet put names.

"We'll go on searching the houses," Pru said, pointing at Storna.

"Make sure you ask before entering," Marko said. Pru shrugged, as if to say that such matters of politeness weren't relevant. "No, really. Someone might be changing their clothes or something."

"I know everyone here." Pru said it with a sneer and put her nose in the air.

"Bokka, will you help me search the paths and the top of the beach?" Laki asked, ignoring this show of superiority. So long as they searched, she didn't care about the niceties.

For a moment, she thought Bokka was going to refuse, but then the young woman nodded. "I'll help."

Chapter 4

THEY WALKED DOWN THE PATH TO THE BEACH slowly. Laki tried to look systematically, both sides of the path, checking everywhere. Bokka mostly gazed out to sea, and Laki started to wonder why she'd chosen Bokka to help. Pru might be annoying, but at least she was actually searching.

"Did you make it a long time ago?" Bokka asked suddenly.

"Not really—last year and over the winter," Laki said. She stopped walking so she could talk without missing any search spots. It took Bokka a few steps to notice, then she had to hurry back to where Laki was standing.

"I wondered because you said that the string might have broken," Bokka explained. "If it was old, it's more likely that something wore out."

"I see what you mean," Laki said. "I don't think it's very likely, but it is possible. If you see a bead on its own which might be from the necklace, you'll let me know?"

Bokka paused. Laki had expected her to say 'yes' or 'of course,' but it seemed that things might not be that straightforward. Then Bokka shook her head. "I remembered something I need to do in my house," she said. "You go on down towards the beach and I'll catch up soon."

She didn't wait for an answer but took off running back to the village. Laki watched her long legs and strong arms moving, puzzled but also intrigued; she felt that Bokka was friendly one moment and fearful the next, helpful for a little while then withdrawing—literally running away—soon after. Perhaps she should have found it off–putting. She knew lots of stories about people who were strange like that and turned out to be untrustworthy, and Heln had coached the whole party on making sure they presented themselves as safe people to ensure good trading relationships. Bokka would make a terrible trader. Nevertheless, Laki felt strongly she wanted to get to know Bokka better.

Bokka reached the village and disappeared, and when she was out of sight, Laki remembered that she was supposed to be looking for something. Half–heartedly, she went on searching along the path, looking first to her left and then her right, taking only a few steps forward at a time. She knew the necklace wasn't here. She ran over the events again in her mind: she'd taken it off to go swimming and left it with her clothes; there was no chance, unless an eagle had picked it up, that it was dropped here without human involvement, and if a person had stolen it, surely they would have taken it away and hidden it.

She was almost at the beach, and had mostly given up searching in favour of staring morosely at the sea, when Sal came up to her. He'd been walking along the shore, he explained, having been sent up to the cliffs in the course of the sheep search, and found the eggs of a seabird up there. He had two eggs now nestled in a fold of his tunic. "Did they find it?" he asked.

"No," Laki said. "I'm going down to the beach in case I missed it last night, with the sun so low."

"Oh, your necklace? No, I meant the sheep, did they find it?"

"Yes!" Laki told him a brief version of the finding in the wood and how Klamro, who was clearly better known to the sheep than many of the other villagers, had been able to catch it because it trusted em.

"Great!" Sal said. "Now, do you want me to help in the necklace hunt as well? I should probably take these eggs to my host so they can be cooked later, but when I've been to the village I can come back." It would be good to have help, and Sal was a familiar face, but... the necklace wasn't there. And Bokka was meant to be with her. Picking up on her hesitation, Sal added, "Or not—or I could send someone else, or...?"

"Bokka was helping me, actually," Laki explained. "She went back to the village, too, to do... something." She hadn't been very clear, Laki realised. Perhaps it was something personal or embarrassing. "If you see her, perhaps you could say you saw me? Or... no, just that. Heln told us not to try and give anyone orders here."

Sal nodded and walked on. Laki watched the sea rising; half a day on from their swimming time, it was at a very similar stage of the tide, creeping up the sand towards the line of seaweed. She strolled back over to the place where they had left their clothes. She looked around, making a spiral out from that point. She didn't really expect to find her necklace, but at least she was moving, and she found it satisfying to imagine the pattern she was making.

The pattern broke when she reached the edge of the water. Her feet were bare anyway and she let the foam run over them before she stepped back. Unusually, she was completely alone. She looked back towards the village but couldn't even see people moving there. There was nobody else on the beach, no one visible in the fields, and no one at the hearth where they had eaten a communal meal the night before.

To distract herself, she stooped and picked up a pretty periwinkle shell. If she had lost one necklace, perhaps it was time to start another; she had seen people drill holes in seashells and could copy them easily enough.

She put another few shells in one of the pouches on her belt. There was still nobody in sight. Not even at the village. She wondered what had happened. It was a fine day, and she would expect to see people working outside—some had probably gone with the sheep and cows, over the hills and into the woods and out of sight, but where were the flint knappers and the wheat grinders and the children playing?

Laki set off towards the village at a quick walk. If something had happened, she wanted to know. Maybe someone was ill, or there'd been an argument.

More likely the latter. As she got closer, she could hear raised voices. "I didn't, I didn't!" Pru was shouting. "I didn't put it there! I didn't even know it was there!"

There was a reply Laki couldn't catch. She started running.

As she reached the entrance to the alley, Bokka said, "We found your necklace."

People filled the space and Laki couldn't see what was happening. "Where was it?" she asked.

Nobody answered but the person in front of her looked over their shoulder, startled, and moved aside. "You'd better go in," they said.

Pru was shouting again. "It's not true, it wasn't me, I didn't do anything!"

"We found it in your bed, Pru." It was Storna speaking. As people saw Laki, they moved aside to let her past, stepping back into their houses or pressing their bodies against the stone walls of the alley, and soon she was at the front. There was a small open area in front of the leader's house, which now felt as constricted as the alley because it was full of people. Inside, she could see Pru, Genu, and Storna, along with more she didn't know.

"I didn't put it there!"

"I'd find it easier to believe you if you hadn't lied to me before." Storna's face was grave, and her voice was low. Genu was watching the two young women, eyes flicking back and forth between them, although he gave a quick and savage grin when he saw Laki arrive.

As they saw her, everyone else started to speak at once. Laki only made out parts of each comment. "We found it—" "I didn't know—" "Bokka said—" "It's not—"

Storna held out the necklace to Laki, and Laki took it. She checked it quickly, not able to see much in the firelight after the bright sunshine but feeling with her fingers the surfaces that she had cut and polished and knew well. All the beads were there, and none were obviously damaged.

A silence fell and Laki realised they were waiting for her reaction. She ran the beads through her hands again, thinking of

Trebbi asking Goddess for guidance, before she looked up. "Thank you for finding it for me," she said.

More noise, and this time Storna won the race to be first and loudest. "It was in Pru's bed, she must have taken it, we can—"

"I didn't do anything!" Pru shrieked.

Laki put the necklace on and teased out her hair with her fingers. "Thank you," she said again. "I don't think we need to do anything else about that now it's found. Genu, I'm sorry I can't help with grinding flour today, but I need to go and see whether Heln has been able to trade our, err, furs."

"Of course, you're a guest, and my daughter will make enough bread for us." It was the first thing Genu had said since she arrived at the house, and Laki wondered what he really made of all this. She didn't linger on the question, though. She held her necklace tightly and left for the open air.

*

After the sheep and the necklace were found, the day went back to almost normal. People hurried to get on with the things they'd planned to do. Klamro was out with the sheep, and Nerto went to pull out weeds from around the beans. "Can you do some flour for tonight?" ey asked Bokka before ey went.

Bokka got herself a bowl full of wheat from the big jar where they kept their supplies and went out to the quern. Aiso was using it, awkwardly and with occasional grunts of pain, so Bokka sat down on a stone nearby to wait. She'd sometimes thought that she should make a new quern for the house. It wouldn't be difficult; you needed to find a big stone with a gentle concave curve to hold the wheat, and a heavy stone which fitted the curve of the other one to rub over it. But Nerto thought it was fine to share with other houses. Although it was slow, Bokka liked the arrangement because it often meant, like today, that there was a break in the day when she was waiting and could simply sit and either listen to the conversation flowing around her or work on carving a little project like an axe-head or a stone ball.

The conversation wasn't flowing, though. Aiso was on his own, and he ground wheat very slowly. "You have a go, lass," he said when he stopped for a rest and realised that Bokka was sitting there. "I can put mine back in my bowl."

Bokka shook her head. "Leave it, and I'll do enough for both of us."

She liked Aiso. He was calm and practical, and even though he was more than fifty summers old, he spoke to her as an equal. His partner had died two winters ago—she'd been even older than him, something Bokka found difficult to imagine—and since then he'd been living with his son's family. Bokka thought his son and his granddaughter ought to do more to help, but Aiso often seemed to end up grinding his own flour.

"You're good at that," Aiso said now, as Bokka took the grinding stone and set her strong shoulders into a suitable rhythm.

"I get a lot of practice."

"So do I, but I seem to be getting weaker instead of stronger," Aiso reflected. He didn't sound bitter, merely thoughtful.

"Doesn't that upset you?" Bokka asked. Then she thought that Klamro would have said that was rude, but it was too late to change her mind.

Aiso leaned back against the low stone Bokka had been sitting on. He didn't seem bothered by the question. "Not really," he said. "It's simply the way of things that I get older and weaker as the summers pass—we are born, and grow, and age, and die. Like the tides rise and fall, and the wheat grows and is cut and ground to flour, and traders visit then disappear again."

"Yes, I suppose so." Bokka didn't usually think of it in long stretches like that. She thought of things in short bursts – her growing, and changing, and wanting to finish a stone ball and start making a necklace and find someone who would love her. She ground for a while longer, slow, firm pushes of the stone across the wheat, moving it with her fingers now and then to keep an even spread. Aiso was quiet, and she thought he might even be dozing off to sleep. "Have you seen lots of groups of traders come and go, then? I've only ever known the little group who come from Sheep Village every year. I didn't know people moved further than that."

"Oh, some people go a long way."

"I can tell that Heln has come a very long way," Bokka said, "because ey has that funny way of making T and D sounds. But the others haven't come so far."

"Otter Village is a fair way, although they are indeed much closer than Heln's place of birth," Aiso agreed. "I even went to Otter Village myself, when I was young and adventurous, and over to the bigger land beyond that island, where they have much thicker forests and bears steal their sheep."

"What are those?"

"Imagine a wolf, but bigger, and able to stand up like a human as well as walk on all fours," Aiso explained. "Like..." He paused, perhaps searching for a comparison which would make sense to someone who had only ever lived on an island too small to support such predators. "Like a walrus, but on legs like a dog. And it eats animals—it would eat a sheep or a cow, or even you."

Bokka shivered at that thought. "I'm glad it didn't eat *you,*" she said. "Do you need enough flour for your family? Or only for you?"

"If you wouldn't mind doing plenty..." Aiso looked tired and Bokka nodded. "It's all very well having lots of shared meals while the traders are here, but it always seems to me that we provide more food than we'd need at home."

"That doesn't make sense." Bokka swept out some fine flour into a bowl and added another handful of wheat grains to the quern. "Everyone is supposed to bring food – it ought to be the same food you'd eat at home, or maybe shared out differently, but it shouldn't be more."

Aiso shrugged. "That's the theory, isn't it? But in practice, someone brings meat to roast, and the rest of us are expected to bring bread, but to go round the people who brought the meat, it has to be extra bread from the households which bring bread. And the meat we cut into shares the last time we butchered an animal sits at home and might be wasted unless we've managed to smoke or salt it."

Bokka had never thought it through like that, but Aiso's explanation made sense. "So we should stop having communal meals?"

"Well, that's for Genu to say, not me."

"Some people would have to feed the traders in their homes."

"It could be a different household each day," Aiso suggested. "It would be less work if we took turns, and we'd all get to meet them properly."

"I've met them."

"But not to sit down and talk over a meal, I think."

Aiso was right. Bokka had assumed that was her failing – the traders had been present at communal meals and she hadn't found the right way to get into the conversation, or Pru had chased her out – but maybe there was more to it. "It would be nice to hear more of their stories."

"Things weren't always like this." Bokka hadn't thought they were, but she kept quiet, focusing on the rhythm of the grinding and waiting to see where Aiso was going. "When I was young, perhaps your age – how old are you now?"

"This is my twentieth summer."

"Yes, about that—when I was your age, I remember a party of traders coming, and they all slept in skin tents outside the village, and visited a different house every day for their food, and helped in the fields as well."

"These traders helped with searching for that sheep that got lost in the woods."

"True. But then one of them lost her necklace as well, and we had to do even more searching."

"She didn't really lose it," Bokka said before the more cautious part of her brain caught up with her mouth and she snapped it shut.

"Same difference; we still had to look for it," Aiso reasoned. "And it was dropped in the very house she was staying in. I don't know why she couldn't find it there herself. Maybe because she's so young."

"She's only the same age as me." That seemed safe enough to say. Bokka cast around for some other topic before this one turned into more trouble. Aiso sounded frustrated with Laki for causing a search, and it gave Bokka a painful, squeezing feeling in her chest. She almost wanted to tell him that it wasn't Laki at all, that the necklace had been stolen, that she'd wanted people to be angry with Pru instead. "Anyway," she said, taking a deep breath and letting the quern stone rest for a moment, "is it true dead people used to be put in trees for the birds, long ago, before we started sending them to sea?"

Aiso laughed. "I'm not that old, you know. But I did hear those stories when I was young, yes, much as you have. Personally, I always thought the sea was good enough for me – it gives us so much, and it's the way to reach so many places, that it makes sense to send people on their way under the sea when they have had enough time on the land. I suppose this was prompted by all Genu's talk about stone buildings for dead people?"

"He says it would be a bit like a house, but different." Bokka bent to her task again, wrinkling her nose. "I can't really imagine it."

"Me neither," Aiso agreed. "And I'm probably closer to it than you are!"

*

For a long time, nothing seemed to be happening. Heln and Marko and Laki had gone with Rika and Wi to sit in a grassy spot near the top of the beach, and Genu had soon joined them. Marko spread out the axe-heads from the bag on a piece of leather. Everyone could see them, and sometimes someone would pick one up, stroke it, feel the edge, look at the colours from different angles, and put it down again.

Rika had a couple of pots by her side. One was large, not the largest Laki had ever seen but big enough to cook evening stew for five or six people, and the other one was small, palm–sized, perhaps for mixing herbs. Somehow, they were going to exchange some axe-heads for some pots, perhaps some pots which hadn't been made yet.

When Laki set out to find Heln and see how the trading worked, she had thought they would simply discuss the goods and what each was worth. What she was hearing didn't seem to arrive at that point. Like hunters gradually getting closer to a deer, it moved slowly and softly, not running straight to the destination but circling around it.

Wi had many questions about the axes. He made axe-heads himself, when there was a demand in the village, and he had thoughts about all aspects of the craft: the best materials, the best polishing methods, how to get the best shape, the best cutting edge, the best shine. To Laki, it was simply boring work which she did on winter evenings before she was allowed to make a bead for her necklace; to Wi, it was obviously a passion.

Marko answered all his questions. Then he asked Rika lots of similar questions about pots—shapes and materials, decorative patterns and uses, and how long they lasted.

Not absorbed in the detail, Laki found herself looking around. It was clearly going to be some time before they got to the questions about trading which interested her—how could you decide how many pots of what size were equivalent to how many axe-heads of which stone? And she couldn't exactly ask them about the other things which were on her mind, like how her necklace had ended up in Pru's bed. She didn't like Pru, but she didn't think the young woman was a liar, and besides, at the time the necklace disappeared, Pru had been in the sea right alongside her. Someone else must have done it, but who? And why?

She imagined someone unknown in the village being so captivated by her special necklace that they absolutely had to handle it. The shine on the tusk–shaped pendants had called to them. The carefully polished beads and the beautiful symmetry of the way they were strung – all of the art and effort which Laki had poured into making it—was irresistible to... someone.

50

"... and Laki helped," Marko said, startling her back into the present. He was holding out an axe-head, which Laki remembered she had worked on, polishing it absentmindedly while thinking of other things. In the sunshine, it looked better than she had thought.

She nodded at him, not sure what other contribution the conversation needed. There was a pause before Marko continued, "You can see for yourselves it's taken on a very fine shine."

The sun moved across the sky. Laki tried to pay attention. It was easier for a while when they got up and went to see the spot where Rika had her fires and she showed them her latest pots. Laki had tried her hand at basic pottery, making simple shapes with clay from the steambed, but not many of her efforts had been good enough to fire and most of those which were shattered in the process, leaving only fragments. She could see that Raki was much more skilled. Some of the pots seemed to transcend their ordinary uses—although they would be useful—and were beautiful in their own right, like the axe-heads which people carried simply for show and not to cut wood.

When it was time to stop and eat, Genu invited them to another communal feast. He'd ordered a calf killed earlier in the day and they would have fresh meat again. Laki was a bit shocked, because Trebbi would have said that they should keep a healthy animal at least until hungry period in the winter, but Heln shrugged and said, "Different villages have different traditions."

It was very pleasant to sit in the sun, in the sea breeze, with nothing much to do. Laki watched a young woman help an older man carry baskets of freshly cooked bread up from the village and recognised Bokka. She saw a chance to hear a different perspective on life in Cow Village and get to know someone intriguing. She waved to Bokka. "Would you like to come and sit with me?"

Chapter 5

BOKKA WASN'T EXPECTING THE INVITATION and at first, she didn't respond. She kept on the path she'd planned, carrying her baskets of bread over to the fire, to a spot where she could put them down with the other baskets and people could easily help themselves or pass the food around. When she did realise what Laki had said, she wondered whether she'd left it too late. Would Laki already be insulted that she'd been ignored? Would someone else already have taken the place? But Bokka wanted it, and instead of pretending that she hadn't heard at all, she turned around slowly, scanning the circle as if looking for a place to sit.

There was nobody in the space next to Laki. Laki was sitting at one end of a big tree trunk which had been cut in half. Bokka thought it had been intended to become a canoe, but the village had lost interest in the project at some stage. There would be room for three or four people to sit close together on the log, but at the moment, Laki was alone.

She was looking up. She was looking at Bokka. Bokka focussed on a point on the top of Laki's head, somewhere in her tightly wound brown curls, and tried a small smile.

"If you'd like to?" Laki said. She gestured at the space next to her.

If Pru had said that, it would have been a trick. Bokka looked at the space on the roughly carved tree trunk but saw nothing terrible there – only wood, no rotten limpet or handful of cow shit or anything else horrible. Perhaps Laki was really being friendly. She was wearing her necklace again, and the polished bone looked warm against her skin.

Bokka sat down.

"Have you been busy today?" Laki asked.

"There was lots to do after this morning," Bokka said. "Usually if it's my turn to grind the flour I start that as soon as I've eaten in the morning so that's it done by the time the sun is high and I can go and help in the fields or collect limpets or look for mushrooms or something."

"But today you had to help with searching for things."

And work out where to hide them. Bokka didn't want to talk about that, so she asked, "Did you know that in other places there are big, hungry animals which live on land and might even eat people? Bears and wolves?"

"I have heard," Laki said. Somewhat late, Bokka realised that the shift in topic would have been too much for some people, but Laki seemed to be coping. "Heln told us a story about a time when ey and eir aunt, Aleuks, were sleeping on the shore near their boat and a bear got into their supplies. They had dried meat and honey to trade, but they traded it to the bear for their lives."

"Didn't they try and chase it off?"

"Apparently Aleuks said it would get angry, so they waited, and at dawn they sailed on as soon as they could."

Bokka nodded solemnly. She was trying to picture a bear – was it shaped like a dog, or a person? Aiso had said it was covered in brown fur...

"You could ask em if you want to hear the whole story," Laki added.

She couldn't really see herself talking to Heln, but she nodded anyway because she guessed that was what Laki wanted her to do. They needed something else to talk about, because the meat wasn't going to be ready for a while. Whoever brought wood for the fire had made some bad choices and it wasn't burning very well. Through the hum of other conversations, Bokka could hear Genu telling someone off about it. The sharp, cross tone of his voice was distinctive – and familiar. She shivered.

"You could move closer to the fire," Laki said. Bokka frowned at her. "If you're cold. Now the sun's going down the breeze has picked up, hasn't it?"

"Yes," Bokka said, but she was puzzled. "I'm not cold."

"You shivered," Laki pointed out. "I only guessed."

"Oh." Interesting – Laki was obviously watching her closely, to notice a detail of that sort. "No, I didn't shiver because I'm cold. I'm just... my hearing is good, and I could hear... someone else talking. It bothered me." Then, remembering the way other people had sometimes responded to this sort of remark, Bokka added, "It's nothing you need to worry about."

"I see." Laki nodded slowly. Nerto was helping to stir the fire, bringing the embers to the top and adding new wood in places where the flames wouldn't damage the pieces of meat roasting on sticks above it. Bokka couldn't see Klamro but she hoped neither of her parents would come and join them. She didn't want to have to talk to anyone except Laki.

In order to do that, though, she would have to keep talking to Laki. She tried to think of a conversation subject and fell back on something Laki had asked earlier. "Have you been busy today?"

Laki scrunched up her face in a strange expression, perhaps a cross between a shrug and a scowl. "Not really." She sighed. "I mean, I had things to do – I spent most of the day listening to people talking about their trading goods. I even talked a little bit myself, about some of the things I made. But mostly I listened to people talking about their pots and their furs and their axes and all that stuff – how things were polished, where the wood came from for the handle, how difficult it is to find the best quality of clay, not any old clay but clay which is really easy to work with. It's kind of interesting, but I'd rather be making things myself."

"What do you like to make?"

"Well..." Laki touched her necklace, and Bokka realised that it had probably been a silly question. Laki was opening her mouth to say more, though, so Bokka kept quiet. "Beads, obviously. I helped with some of the axes we're selling; I'm not so good at the initial work, but I can do the fine polishing, getting them to really shine. I've done some basic pots, but we have other people in Otter Village who specialise in those. I can make some other stone tools, simple knapped flints, things like that."

"I like to polish things, too." Bokka opened her pouch and pulled out the half–finished stone ball she was carrying. "Look, I'm working on this at the moment. The pattern is made by the bumps, you see, and I'm almost finished pecking it out so these six bumps stand away from the surface of the ball."

Laki touched it, and Bokka let her take it from her hand. That was only fair, Bokka thought, since she had handled Laki's necklace. Not that Laki knew that. She had to remember that there were lots of things Laki didn't know. "It's good," Laki was saying, running her fingers around one of the most finished sections.

"It's not complicated," Bokka said, taking it back and managing to brush her fingers against Laki's in the process. They felt nice, warm with not too much rough skin. "I've got a plan to make a more elegant one, with lots of small knobs instead of these six flat disks, but I need to finish this one first."

"It'll look good when it's polished." Laki was very close, her shoulder brushing Bokka's. "It'll feel good to touch it." Bokka glanced at her, not her face, but her throat, where those warm fingers were now touching the smooth surfaces of her necklace again. The bone beads would be warm against her skin. The fire was warm on Bokka's face, too. She was not cold at all. She was too hot. She didn't know what to say. Her cheeks felt as if they were glowing embers. Laki was still talking. "I'd like to see it when it's finished. I think it'll be lovely."

Bokka nodded. She wanted to speak but had to swallow. Her throat was suddenly dry.

"Some of this is ready to eat," Nerto said loudly nearby. "Those who are here might as well start, Genu. We'll move the other pieces of meat into the middle of the fire and hopefully it'll be ready when the others come in from the fields."

After that, Laki's attention was all on the food. She hadn't moved much but Bokka could see her foot out, ready to go and collect her share. Bokka had been starting to prepare an answer about the polishing process or the stone ball. It now seemed too late.

They ate the bread she'd baked. She'd helped Aiso for almost the whole day. They'd baked the two sets of bread together, chatting, Aiso working on a new tunic, then swapping the round, flat loaves over on the hot stones of Aiso's hearth.

She'd also popped out and got something to replace the necklace for the night.

As she watched Laki turn to Sal to ask something about the animals they'd be interested in trading for, Bokka reminded herself that she didn't need to keep Laki's attention all the time, even when she'd briefly enjoyed it. She had plenty of different ways to be close to her.

*

The bed space seemed empty. It took Laki a moment to examine the stone sides, the pillow full of feathers, the leather bag she had left there, her winter cloak, and realise what was missing: one of the heavy furs Pru had given her. It was warm enough in the house and she might not really need it. She considered simply going to sleep but thought it would seem strange to notice now and not ask until the morning.

"Pru?"

The other woman turned from where she was shaking out a fur of her own, ready to get into bed. "What?"

"Sorry, I wondered – you gave me a fur the other day, the big one, I think it was from a deer. I'm sure it was here this morning, but I can't see it now."

"Oh, Goddess," Pru moaned. "Help us, help us. Yet another thing is missing. Is it today? Is today a day of things going to the wrong places? Or is it something I've done? Has one of the ancestors taken against me and come back as a ghost to hide things and give me the most uncomfortable day possible?"

Laki didn't know what to say to that, so she simply watched Pru go through all these possibilities. If anything, Laki thought that she had been more targeted than Pru; why would Pru's ancestors take a sheep which had nothing to do with her, and Laki's necklace, and the sleeping fur Laki had been using? If anyone had annoyed a ghost, it was probably Laki.

Annoyed ghosts weren't her main worry, though. She thought her ancestors were sleeping peacefully, in their well–built tomb or the deep channel between Otter Village and the next piece of land. Pru, however, was obviously not sleeping peacefully, and Laki wasn't going to get any sleep at all if she didn't sort this out somehow.

"I didn't touch your fur," Pru continued. "I don't know why you're asking *me*. I didn't take your necklace, I don't know how it can possibly have ended up in my bed, I didn't take your fur back even though it was sort of mine anyway, it isn't on my bed, you can check!" She stepped aside and made a large, pointing gesture to show that Laki could look for herself.

"I believe you," Laki said, not moving. She didn't want to start a search. She didn't want to annoy someone she had to share a house with. "I wondered whether you'd seen it, that's all. I could have put it down in the wrong place this morning because we were all in a rush, getting out to look for that sheep."

"Hmm." This explanation seemed to have calmed Pru a lot. She picked up a scallop shell lamp with a little animal fat in it and lit the wick from the fire. "Here, let's have a look around with this to help us."

They started around Laki's bed, then Genu's, then Pru's, then the empty space where Pru said her mother had slept before she died. There was no sign of the fur Laki had been using, but there were plenty of others. "People bring them to Genu as presents," Pru explained when Laki commented on them. "It's good if the leader has plenty, because he might be asked to take in guests or to provide something warm for people to wrap up in. When we have to have a big meeting in the winter, sometimes so many people come it still has to be outside, and we use all the furs we can find. So if someone ever has a spare one, it tends to end up here. And we have some good leather workers who manage to process the furs from a lot of our kills, so there often are spares."

That all made sense. Laki said she would use one of the others tonight.

"We'll look for the other one in the morning," Pru said. "It might have been a gift, but it should have stayed here."

"Perhaps someone needed it," Laki suggested as she finally curled up to sleep.

"They should have asked," Pru muttered before there was silence.

*

Laki stirred at some point in the night – she thought she heard someone moving and guessed Genu had come in – but otherwise she slept deeply and undisturbed, one hand tucked under her cheek and the other touching her necklace.

The next day seemed quiet and uneventful. As they ate their morning food, Genu was talking about tomb building again. He had simply shrugged when told about the missing fur, and said there were so many, maybe Laki didn't recognise it. Much more important was today's visit to the proposed tomb location. He wanted Sal's opinion on it, and they would pray there and see whether it got good omens.

Laki nodded, still stung by being told she couldn't tell the difference between one fur and another, and didn't say anything. She wasn't sure what omens they would be looking for, anyway. What would be appropriate for a tomb? To arrive at the place you planned to build it and find that a sheep had already dropped dead on the spot?

She kept that thought to herself and went on nodding while Genu and Pru went through, again, the two different designs they were considering.

There didn't seem to be anything much else to do. She could have gone to help in the fields – there were always weeds to pull out from between the beans and so on – or she could have tried to make a trade of her own, or offered to help Pru with grinding the day's flour – but what she really wanted to do was work on a necklace made of shells, and she couldn't really do that. Most of her tools were at home, including the stone point she'd made specially for drilling. Besides that, she worried that if she started making something new while she was here, people would assume it was intended for trading, and she rather wanted to be able to keep it. If it turned out well. If it wasn't what she imagined, perhaps she would trade it away after all.

Genu was about to set off. "Are you grinding wheat with me?" Pru was asking.

Laki shook herself out of her thoughts. "I'll go with Genu, if that's okay. I'd like to see this tomb–building space."

"What do you know about tombs?" Genu asked. "I didn't ask for your opinion."

Actually, she thought he had asked all the guests, and Sal and Heln had had their opinions taken seriously, but she didn't want to argue. Instead, she shrugged. "I guess I can help with the flour instead."

"You don't have to spend time with me if you don't want to," Pru said. She sniffed, which could have been a check that the grain she was fetching was still good, or a comment on Laki's behaviour.

Laki didn't really want to. She tried to think of something else which might be a reasonable activity but felt empty handed.

Genu ignored all this and gave Pru some final instructions for the day – what should be cooked for later, messages to pass on to others in the village, what to do when the flour was ground – before hurrying out.

Pru got on with her work. Not sure what else to do, Laki sat on the bed and watched. When Pru left the house, Laki followed. They didn't speak.

When they got to the querns, Bokka was using the largest one. Aiso was sitting nearby and they were talking; Bokka was explaining all about polishing materials, especially the benefits of using sand from a particular beach nearby. Pru went to a smaller quern which had an uneven side and started on her flour.

"You don't have to use that, I'll be done soon," Bokka said when she finished her previous point.

"I just need to get it done," Pru said. She pushed her grinding stone forward so violently that some of the wheat grains flew out of the front. She picked up one or two and left the others there, wasted.

Bokka glanced up and spotted Laki. "Are you helping, too?"

"I could be," Laki said. At that moment, she was uncomfortably aware that she was not helping, not even wanted for help, but simply stood while others worked because she didn't know what to do and hadn't been given a role.

"You could try this quern," Bokka said, pointing at a stone with a very shallow bowl scooped out of it. "I know it's small but it works well enough – I found this new grinding stone on the beach the other day and it fits perfectly, so it should be efficient."

Laki lifted the grinding stone Bokka had indicated and saw that it was indeed exactly the right shape. She wouldn't be able to grind much at a time in the little bowl, but what she did grind should become a very fine flour and quickly, too. She turned to Pru to ask for a handful of grain to start on, but Pru scowled at her and moved the bowl away.

"This is for my family and Aiso's," Bokka said, pushing a large bowl of wheat towards Laki.

"Happy to help," Laki said. She took a small handful and got started.

They worked in uncomfortable silence for a while. Aiso made one or two comments, but when the others didn't answer or only said, "Ah," or "Is that so?" he soon gave up.

Laki added her flour to the pile in Bokka's other bowl. Pru rushed through hers, scattering more around the quern and leaving some of it rather roughly ground. *Genu will complain about the bread tonight,* Laki thought. Nobody said anything. The grinding stones made their own sounds, the rough scrape of one surface against another and some knocking or tapping sounds as they cleaned flour off a surface or moved the stone to a better position.

Eventually, Pru left. Bokka and Laki kept working on the big pile in Bokka's bowl; it was from Aiso's family as well, Laki had worked out.

"We'll do extra and you can eat with us tonight," Bokka said when Pru had gone.

"Thank you."

"And don't mind Pru," Aiso added. "And won't Genu want to do the big feast thing again?"

Bokka sighed. "I know it's summer but we don't need to be doing that all the time. It means we never get to eat fish or anything. And I worry that if we have too many roast meat meals now there won't be enough animals left for the winter. Or to breed."

"And it's too much to do to process all the skins, and we aren't even using all the bones properly," Aiso added.

Laki kept grinding flour, pushing back and forth over the quern, and listened to this with fascination. She'd noticed that things were very different here. At home, big communal meals were reserved for times when there needed to be a big meeting, for the whole community to talk something through, hear the voice of Goddess, and make a decision, but she hadn't realised that it wasn't normal for Cow Village, either.

"I don't even know why Genu's doing it." Bokka took a little break from her work, stretched her shoulders, and shook her head. "Does he really like roast meat that much? Or is he trying to avoid Pru's cooking?"

"I think he's trying to show off to our guests," Aiso said. Laki glanced at him and when he caught her eye, he gave her a mischievous grin. "He wants them to think that we're incredibly well off here, that we've got loads of stuff and we can afford to eat huge meals every day, and nobody has to go and collect limpets or anything like that. Not that our huge pile of limpet shells wouldn't give them a clue, even if tactless people like me weren't blabbering about the whole situation in front of them."

"I'm sure you're being very polite and helping me understand the local tradition," Laki said. Aiso laughed.

"Of course we're being nice to you," Bokka said. Laki thought she had picked up some of the sarcastic tone but not understood the whole joke. "We ought to be very nice to you because you might trade lovely things with us, and anyway, Pru and them aren't very good at it."

"They've mostly been polite to me," Laki said, wanting to be fair, "until today. But I have seen they're not always nice to you, and although I've been staying in Pru and Genu's house, I haven't actually eaten very much of their cooking. Is it known to be bad?"

It was, and Aiso and Bokka spent some time filling Laki in about disasters past – burned meals, horrible smells, food left to rot, needing to ask others in the village for help. The stories weren't nice but they were told to be amusing, and the conversation kept them busy while they finished the work of grinding the wheat. When the bowl of grain was empty, they took the flour to Aiso's house. He made dough while Bokka and Laki looked around.

"Are your houses like this?" Bokka asked.

"Very similar." Laki described her family home, with the shelves and the hearth and the sealed water–box for keeping shellfish fresh like Aiso's.

"I usually try and keep ours full," Bokka said. "My favourite food is mostly seafood. Limpets. Crab. Lobster. Whale meat, seal meat, when we can get it."

"Mmm, crab," Laki said. Her mouth watered. "I like crab. I used to go and catch crabs in the rock pools near our village when I was young. I haven't had time to do that for ages."

"We could go today," Bokka said. "Aiso, do you need us for anything else? We could go round to where the rocks are exposed at low tide and find some crabs. We'll bring you some if there are lots."

"Thank you for your help with the flour," Aiso said. He straightened up slowly and with a groan. "No, I'll be fine from here. The dough will rise. I'll go and see if I can help with the weeding or something. My son won't be far away, probably in the bean field. Enjoy your crabbing. Remember to take a big jar with steep sides so they can't climb out again!"

Grinning, Bokka made a pinching movement with her hand, imitating a crab's claw.

Chapter 6

THE TIDE WAS STILL GOING OUT as Bokka and Laki reached the rocks around the headland. Laki had seen them from the boat as they entered the bay, but not since, and she followed more carefully as Bokka climbed and scrambled over them. They went barefoot for better grip, although some of the barnacles were rough and the rocks could be sharp. Bokka knew the rockpools well and the first crab was in the jar before Laki had got her eye in to search for the little scuttling creatures in the rocks and shallow water.

"You can balance the jar here," Bokka said, showing Laki a flat space with a jutting rock above it on which the jar could lean at a slight angle but was unlikely to fall anywhere. They used their hands to scoop in a little sea water to keep the crabs alive and fresh, then set about their hunt.

Bokka quickly found two more crabs and came back to the jar with one in each hand. More cautious and less familiar with the area, Laki hadn't gone far. "The tide will turn soon." Bokka nodded out to sea.

"It'll take a while to reach here, though," Laki said.

"Yes, but I want to go further out. There will be more to find in the places which aren't uncovered for so long."

"Ah." Laki felt she was meant to be pulling out some implication from this, but it wasn't reaching her.

"So," Bokka said, deliberately patient, "can you bring the jar? I don't want to have to come back here every time I've caught two."

"Err... yes." Carefully, Laki stepped back to the jar and picked it up. She was anxious about slipping on the seaweed–

covered rocks, especially closer to the sea where they hadn't been drying for so long. "How many are we after?"

Bokka shrugged. "As many as we can find. Eight, maybe? Eight would be good. If we eat one each, that's you and me and my parents and Aiso and Aiso's son and a couple to give away or save for tomorrow. One crab this size is a good meal. I don't like sharing them."

"Okay, let's try." Laki felt awkward following Bokka's nimble steps over the rocks, and not only because she was carrying the jar as well as trying not to slip. There was a lot demanding her attention: the rocks, her feet, the jar, Bokka's feet, Bokka's hips, the confident way she hopped across the uneven ground, the relaxation in her shoulders now they were away from the village. Laki liked to see it and she watched appreciatively – but only for a moment, because her toes slid across a patch of seaweed and she had to jerk her focus back to her own balance before she fell.

By the time the waves began to come up the rocks towards them, they had seven crabs and Bokka said they should turn around. "We might find one we missed on the way back, but we don't want to get washed into the sea here."

"No – one thing to swim by the sandy beach..."

"A few years back a man was killed because the waves washed him off these rocks." Bokka didn't say it dramatically, simply as a fact, but the image still made Laki shiver and pay renewed attention to her steps. Bokka was carrying the jar now, and Laki had begun to feel more confident to choose the safe places to put down her feet. Not anymore. There wouldn't be any blood left to see, of course, but Laki's imagination was happy to fill it in. A body swept back against the rocks and thrown down on these sharp points.

She'd stopped walking. Bokka looked back. "Are you okay?"

Laki took a deep breath. She could smell seaweed and salt, the normal scents of the water's edge. "Yes," she said. "Yes, sorry, I was resting for a moment. I'm coming." She hurried after Bokka.

When they were off the rocks, Bokka led the way onto the headland. They were out of sight of the village, with a band of trees as well as a short walk separating them from the places people tended to gather, and at the top of the cliff Bokka showed Laki a place where they could sit on some soft grass and look out at the sea.

"People think I'm wasting my time, but I like watching it move."

"No more wasting your time than making something with no practical use," Laki replied. She touched her necklace, a project she'd been told many times to leave because something more urgent needed doing.

"They won't even know we aren't still hunting for crabs."

"They'll be glad we're hunting for something new instead of something lost." Bokka didn't reply and after a moment Laki felt prompted to ask, "Do things go missing a lot in Cow Village?"

"What do you mean?" Bokka gave her a swift but piercing glance. Criticisms of Cow Village, Laki suspected, would not be taken well.

"There was the sheep, obviously, but that can happen anyway," Laki said. "But my necklace went missing, and I never did work out how it ended up in Pru's bed. She couldn't have taken it, because she was swimming with me when it went missing. And last night the fur I'd been sleeping under had gone. Genu and Pru have lots, so it didn't matter, but it puzzled me."

"I took it."

"What?" Laki turned to fully face Bokka. "What do you mean?"

Bokka covered her face with her hands. She hadn't meant to say that aloud. She had been trying not even to think it.

"What do you mean you took it?" Laki asked again. "Bokka, did you really take the fur off my bed?"

Time for truths. Bokka blurted, "It had touched you."

She risked a glance at Laki's face, often not as useful a move as she would have liked, and sure enough, she couldn't interpret Laki's expression. Was that a frown of anger or confusion? Was she about to shout? Pru would have been shouting by now, and Bokka's hands twitched towards her ears.

Laki was not shouting. Not yet. She had taken a deep breath, but then paused, and when she opened her mouth she said, "That's true, it had touched me."

It was Bokka's turn to be confused. She tried to keep explaining, almost hoping that Laki would be angry soon. That might be easier than understanding. "I know it was wrong. I shouldn't take your things. I shouldn't have taken your necklace. I wanted to feel it, so I picked it up, but then I was worried that Genu and the others would see me, so I took it back to my house, and it felt so smooth... it's really nice. You made it really well."

There was another silence, in which Bokka tried to think of what else to say, and Laki's face went through several complicated expressions. One of them was definitely a bad expression, with a wrinkled forehead. The last one seemed to be in between, maybe even neutral or blank. People sometimes said that Bokka looked blank, even when she was listening or thinking very hard, and perhaps she looked like that.

"Thank you," Laki said eventually. "I worked hard on it. I wished you'd asked me, because I was very upset when I didn't know where it was, and I would have let you hold it. But the fur wasn't anything special, I didn't make it, but you took that, too."

"Yes." Laki was being very plain and clear, or it felt like it. Bokka hoped it was for real. "When I'd put your necklace back—"

"In Pru's bed," Laki interrupted.

Bokka shrugged. "She deserves to be in trouble sometimes."

"I think she's in trouble often enough." Bokka shrugged again, because she didn't agree but it seemed to be off the main point of the conversation, and Laki sighed. "Anyway, you put my necklace in Pru's bed, and she found it and gave it back to me. And then..."

"Then I really missed it during the night." Perhaps that didn't convey the full extent of what she'd felt, the sense of something having been taken away from her, the way only thinking about Laki could fill the space left behind, but Bokka didn't know how to put anymore into words. "I had liked the way it made me feel... close to you. I wanted that again. So while you were out, I went and..." It was hard to say, but Laki didn't move when she paused and Bokka managed to keep going. "And took the fur off your bed."

The breeze was picking up and Bokka gazed out to sea, watching the tops of the waves begin to turn white, as she waited for Laki to answer.

"I think I understand," Laki said. "You wanted to feel my necklace, and then you wanted to be near me, so you took the fur. What I would still like to know is... how do you feel now? We're sitting up here, away from the village, alone – apart from the crabs, and they're in a jar. You're near me. You're close enough to touch me if you want to. Do you want to?"

Bokka couldn't move. She was overwhelmed by a rush of different answers. She felt relaxed up here, and worried about what Laki would do next, and guilty about stealing things, and uncertain about her own feelings. She wanted to touch Laki, and she wanted Laki to touch her, and she wanted it to be warm and not in this cool breeze, and she wanted to see Laki's skin and wrap Laki up in the fur and look after her. She looked around and discovered that Laki was indeed very close. Either they'd sat down closer together than Bokka remembered, or Laki had moved closer while they'd be talking.

"It's usual to ask, you know, once you've got me alone," Laki said.

But Bokka didn't know, and she shook her head. Laki had been leaning even closer but now moved slightly back.

"I'm sorry I took your necklace and your fur," Bokka said. Not yet sure what she felt about the rest of the conversation, she went back to an earlier theme. "Aren't you angry? It's been years since I took anything else which belonged to someone, but normally there's shouting at least. Sometimes hitting. Telling me I'm never welcome in their house again." Laki's face had changed. "Yes, angry like that." It was almost a relief to be back on familiar ground.

"No," Laki said firmly. and Bokka's relief flowed away again like rainwater running into the sea. "I'm not angry with you, Bokka. I was confused, and upset, and I was annoyed before I understood what happened, but you've explained. I'm not sure it's the best way to express interest in getting to know someone, but I can see where you were coming from, and Pru and Storna and the others didn't make it easy for us to spend time together to start with. You must have been very curious about me."

That made Bokka smile. She had been drawn to Laki from the first moment the trading party arrived, and Laki's analysis of the situation was spot on.

"So I'm not angry with you. You did do something wrong, but now you've tried to put it right, by putting my necklace somewhere I would find it, and telling me what happened. I am angry but it's with the others. The people who shouted at you and hit you."

Something broke the pattern of the waves, and Bokka watched the sea until she had identified an orca, further out than she could swim. She pointed it out to Laki.

"Imagine if they were as easy to catch as crabs," Laki said.

"We'd make ourselves sick eating their meat for days." But the idea also made Bokka laugh. "We'd never run out."

"I could make hundreds of necklaces with whale–tooth beads."

"I wouldn't have to steal that one." Bokka glanced at it, carefully keeping her longing to touch under control. "And I don't think the people who were cross with me for stealing were wrong, by the way. I hate it when someone else takes something I thought was mine. I didn't want to upset you – or anything. It was just... when I walked past..."

"It made sense to you." Laki's voice was soft. It was as well she was sitting very close by or Bokka might not have heard her over the sound of the waves, now lapping at the base of the cliff.

It had. In the moment, it had made perfect sense; only afterwards had Bokka realised how it would seem to other people.

"Do you like living here?" Laki asked.

"In Cow Village?" Bokka had no immediate answer. She had always lived here, in this village with her parents. She'd made a few short visits to other villages or to the great circles of upright stones, or once to another village where they had built a new tomb and wanted to show it off. She'd never spent this long with someone who wasn't also part of Cow Village. There were things which could change her life – sometimes dramatically, like the death of someone important to her or a big change in the way the village was organised – but she'd always imagined the new life as taking place in the same spot as the old one. Even her fantasy about getting rid of Pru simply had the other young woman disappear while Bokka stayed in the same house.

She couldn't find the words to say all of that to Laki. "I suppose it's nice enough. We've got the sea as well as the fields and the forest. There's always plenty to eat." Bokka indicated their jar, where the crabs could be heard bumping into one another and trying to climb the sides. "Is Otter Village like that?"

Otter Village was a lot like that. Laki nodded, but reluctantly; there were other differences she wanted to put her finger on. "Yes, it's a lot like here as far as food goes – we're close to the sea, and to fresh, inland water, and we have woods and sheep and cows and fields of wheat and all those things. And we have a tomb. I think the difference is... how the people are. In Otter Village we have a leader, but she listens much more to other people."

"We have village meetings," Bokka said. She sounded almost defensive, which Laki thought was strange given how Genu and the others treated her. "Genu calls a village meeting sometimes, like we had one about this thing about building a tomb, and he asked for everyone's ideas."

"And did he act on any of them?"

"No," Bokka admitted.

"And he gave orders when we all had to go out to look for that sheep."

"I suppose your leader would have listened to the sheep's ideas and not let it get lost in the first place?"

Laki laughed. "No, our sheep wander off sometimes, too. I'm sure it happens everywhere. But our leader, Trebbi, probably would have asked Klamro about where ey thought the sheep would be, since it was obvious that Klamro knows the sheep best, and started looking there. And she would have let people volunteer for areas they usually work in, or that they know well, and to work together with their friends or family instead of splitting them up at random."

She sensed Bokka moving away. For a while earlier on she'd thought this conversation might end in a kiss, or even more, and she'd been looking forward to that. But this turn away from Bokka's experience and feelings to comparing their villages, although more lighthearted, clearly wasn't going to be romantic. She tried to bring it back.

"Our village is more open, too, with gaps between the houses. I like the way yours is covered over. It must be lovely and cosy in the winter."

The compliment was meant to bring Bokka's smile back. Instead, Bokka stood up. "We ought to get back. We need time to cook bread and prepare the crabs and things." So much for their newfound closeness. Laki was following Bokka down the path towards the village when Bokka turned back briefly. "You're still welcome to eat with us if you want to. My parents won't mind, and it would be some time away from Genu and Pru if you want it."

Laki's heart leapt with hope again and she worked hard to keep her voice steady and casual when she said, "Thanks, that would be great."

As they prepared for the evening meal, it was interesting to watch the three of them interacting. Bokka's parents asked Laki if she wanted to help, and when she said yes, gave her the simple task of flipping the cakes of bread on the hot stones as each cooked. They even had a pair of specially carved wooden tools for the job. At home, Laki would have improvised with a stick, and perhaps a thick piece of leather, and blown on her hands when they were burnt.

"These are good," she said when she noticed Klamro watching her use them.

Chapter 7

AFTER EATING, LAKI CREPT BACK to Genu's house. She had left the fur with Bokka and declined an offer to sleep in Bokka's house. Although she was sure Nerto and Klamro were genuine in the offer, she really wanted a little time away from Bokka to think. Being near to Pru again might not help, but she managed to get into bed without waking anyone.

It took her a long time to fall asleep because she kept remembering bits of her conversation with Bokka. She swung rapidly between different emotions. Why couldn't other people listen to Bokka and respect her and look after her the way Laki wanted to? So annoying! But also, why did Bokka have to try and get Pru in trouble for the theft – wasn't that making things worse? Bokka had to take some responsibility. And then again, why was Bokka being driven to act like this? Was she more like a dog who wants to be petted, or a sheep who can be persuaded to go almost anywhere with a dog behind, or a bird who startles and flies away at the slightest noise?

Laki wasn't sure any of those comparisons made much sense. In her dreams the crabs got muddled up with boats, little wooden boats she could fish out of rockpools, and Bokka got muddled up with a fur which was covering her. When she woke, she was rubbing her cheek against the soft leather and for a moment she imagined it was Bokka's skin, perhaps Bokka's shoulder, in the bed alongside her.

It wasn't. Laki peeled it away, and stretched a little, and made some little waking–up sounds to warn anyone else in house that she was about to move. When she sat up, though, she realised she was alone. She had been late coming in – she'd heard two sets of breathing, and Genu's occasional snores, so she knew both of them had been there when she arrived – and apparently she'd slept late, too. There was a hunk of yesterday's bread by the banked–in fire, but Genu and Pru must have got up and left without waking her.

That suited her well enough. Laki chewed on the bread and thought about what to do. It was tempting to go and find Bokka again. She would probably be grinding flour as usual, chatting with Aiso. After yesterday, though, Laki thought she might need some time to get her thoughts in order. She wanted to spend time with Bokka – had thought they were going to kiss and welcomed the idea – but she also wanted to help. Bokka was clearly struggling with some parts of life, especially how to connect with other people. If Laki had been in her position, wouldn't she have found another way, a non–stealing way, to get close to her?

Maybe and maybe not. Laki decided to try and find someone of her own to talk to – Heln, if possible, but at least someone who knew Otter Village and a bit more of the world.

When she left the underground part of the village (making sure to go the opposite way to where she thought Bokka would be, at the querns), she found Pru working on a bunch of dandelion roots, cleaning them in a bowl of fresh water and cutting them into small pieces for cooking. She asked where the other traders were.

"Heln and Marko have gone out to the far fields with Genu. They're looking at some wheat which is doing something interesting," Pru twisted her mouth to indicate that this was not her own opinion of the wheat, "and then to find a ram they might want to trade for. But Sal is around somewhere. He was going to get some of the bones from one of last week's kills and make some, err..."

"Probably awls or something," Laki said. "Great, do you know which way he went?"

Pru pointed. Laki followed her directions and found Sal sitting at the top of the beach, not far from where they had left their boat.

74

"Good morning." Sal seemed genuinely pleased to see her. "Care to give me a hand with these? I know you're good at bone–working."

"Of course." She squatted comfortably next to him and took a handful of flint blades from a pouch on her belt. Sal had already split and cleaned several long bones – probably very recently, since there was a dog hovering on the beach in case more marrow appeared. Laki picked a likely–looking piece and began to work a diagonal line which would, if all went well, turn it into the points of two awls.

"I thought you'd be spending time with the locals," Sal said. "You seem to have fitted in well, got to know some people."

Laki shrugged. She didn't feel that way at all, although it was interesting to know how things seemed from Sal's perspective. "I have got to know some of them," she agreed. "But some of them..." She glanced around to check that nobody else was in earshot before continuing, "don't seem to be very nice to each other."

"Everyone has ways to hurt each other," Sal said placidly.

"Not like this!" Laki didn't want to hear that Bokka's situation was like everyone else's. "Pru in particular is nasty to other people." All her observations started to come tumbling out, roaring over her tongue like a river reaching a cliff. She told Sal about the way Pru excluded Bokka from conversations; about the way they couldn't cooperate over something as everyday as grinding flour; and about how Bokka had been left out of the swimming party and needed to get back at Pru by trying to make people think she'd stolen a necklace.

When she eventually run dry, tired and thirsty and desperate for Sal to understand what she was saying, there was a long silence. Sal held up the point he was working on to check that it was smooth and straight.

"You've got very involved with their lives," he said.

"I thought it was good that I'd been getting to know them!"

"It is," Sal assured her. "But I think we won't be staying for much longer. If Heln and Marko really agree a trade for a ram, we'll want to take it and get back to Otter Village soon. He'll need time to recover from the journey and settle in before he's expected to start tupping our ewes."

That was all true and sensible, but it didn't speak to Laki's concerns at all. "Don't you care about how people here treat each other?"

It was Sal's turn to shrug. "I suppose so, but it's not really mine to make decisions about, is it? If they want to treat each other better, they can. If there's really a problem, someone should take it to Genu, or to a village meeting, to be discussed and sorted out with the help of Goddess." He gave Laki an assessing look. "It sounds like you really care about them, though. Or at least about one of them."

Laki's face went hot, which was how she knew he was right. "I suppose I do," she said, trying to pass it off as casual. She pushed too hard on the blade she was using and a much bigger piece of bone than she intended split away from the proto–awl. She pulled it off with a groan. "Shit."

"Smooth it off, it'll still make a small awl."

She was glad Sal was calm and encouraging about that, at least. "I mean, I do care, especially about Bokka. The others here don't seem to value her skills very much." She told Sal about the speed of Bokka's crabbing, which didn't interest him very much, and the way she was making a special carved stone ball, which was closer to his heart and got some questions about her technique. "So I wondered whether she should come with us. Klamro and Nerto and Aiso would miss her, but Genu and Pru would probably be glad to see the back of her, so I don't think she'd have trouble getting permission to leave."

Sal's reaction was not as immediately positive as she'd hoped it would be. "She would still need to check with the village, though – and her parents might object. And we'd have to think she would fit in back in Otter Village – if that many people don't like her here, what if they don't like her there, either? You did say she stole things, which isn't usually popular, even if she has her own strange reasons for it. And Heln and Marko would have to be okay with it, too. She'd have to come on the boat with us – has she ever sailed? And do you even know whether she actually wants to leave?"

Annoyingly, Sal had a point there. "I haven't actually asked her if she'd want to come," Laki admitted. "But could I have asked – without talking to you and Heln and Marko first – what if I'd asked and she'd really wanted to come, and then you'd said no?"

"Then she would be hurt," Sal agreed. He switched tools, finding a flint with a sharp point which he could use to drill a hole through another piece of bone. "And we – Heln in particular – could still say no."

"Do you think ey will?" Laki asked. "Do you think ey *should?*"

"That's really up to em." Sal sighed and gave her a smile which conveyed sympathy but not agreement. "You've started the conversation. Started asking people what's possible. That's probably all you can do at this point."

*

That night, Heln had agreed a trade for not only one but two rams from Cow Village's flock, and Genu insisted they have another communal feast to celebrate. By the time Laki had washed the dust off her hands and face from her day's work making awls and pins, the lamb was already roasting and the bread – which most people had already cooked, assuming they would eat in their own homes – was piled up ready to eat.

There weren't many spaces in the crowd. It seemed that more people had come this time – perhaps because it was a real feast, with something to celebrate, or for some other reason Laki didn't know about – and it wasn't until Heln turned and saw her that she could see a way to find somewhere to sit. Heln and Marko had claimed a patch of ground near the fire, spreading out a fur to sit on. When Heln saw Laki, ey moved across and nudged Marko to move as well until there was space for all three of them. Relived, Laki knelt down. It was good to see them and to feel part of her own community; talking to Sal over their work had left Laki feeling unsettled, and when Aiso had come to join them, and they hadn't been able to carry on the conversation, she had felt a little anxiety all day. What would Heln and Marko really say? Would Bokka want to leave?

Sitting with them, although she couldn't raise the question about Bokka, she felt more included. Heln told her all about the two rams they were taking home, and how they would be good for the stock in Otter Village, and what ey thought Trebbi would say about them. Marko admired one of the awls she had made. The conversation wasn't deep, but it flowed easily. On the other side of Marko, Klamro joined in with a question about the sheep in Otter Village, and they were off, comparing notes about lambing times and food preferences and fleece texture.

Half listening to the chatter about sheep and half thinking about Bokka, Laki looked around the gathered crowd. The roast lamb had been served and most people were eating. She could see Pru sitting next to Storna, their heads bent close together as if for a secret. Pru was wiping grease off her fingers with some bread and looking across the fire with a scowl. Laki followed her gaze and realised that Pru was staring at Bokka.

Bokka was at the back of the crowd, squatting alone and chewing meat off a bone. Her eyes were closed, Laki thought in pleasure, and she was clearly attending only to her own food. Whatever had upset Pru, it wasn't something Bokka was doing in that moment.

Storna laughed, loud enough for Laki to hear over the other noises of eating and talking. As she looked back at them, Pru stood up. She walked over towards Bokka.

Tense, Laki almost stood up herself. She didn't know what was going to happen, but she wanted to be there if Bokka needed help. But Heln's hand was on her shoulder. "We're not here to get caught up in local arguments," ey said softly. "I see you watching, and that's okay, but we're observers here, not the hunters."

Laki took a deep breath and forced herself to relax enough to stay seated. She couldn't bring herself to eat but lifted her meat to her mouth and mimed taking a bite.

At first it seemed fine. Pru touched Bokka's shoulder lightly so that she startled and looked up. Then Pru sat down next to her, in a gesture which looked nothing but friendly. Bokka's body language wasn't happy, though.

Pru was saying something. She was smiling slightly and talking calmly. Laki had no way of knowing what Pru was saying – they were too far away and everyone else around was talking too – but when Laki saw Bokka try to stand up, she knew it couldn't be anything really friendly. Pru didn't let Bokka leave, grabbing her wrist and pulling her back down.

Laki glanced around to see if anyone else was watching this. Nearby, Heln was watching. Perhaps what she had said earlier had drawn eir attention to Bokka. The only other person who seemed to be looking in that direction was Storna, and Laki had to assume that she would be on Pru's side rather than supporting Bokka.

Now Pru was leaning in and whispering, right into Bokka's ear. Bokka looked like she was about to cry.

Laki put her food down. She couldn't let this continue. Walking over to them meant passing lots of other people, twisting around other groups, trying not to step on anyone or their food. People looked up, then followed her gaze to where she was going. Seeing her coming – and the attention which came with it – Pru quickly stood as well. By the time Laki got there, Pru had shot her last arrow, whatever it was, and was walking away. She deliberately bumped Laki's shoulder, making it look like an accident as they both passed a small child struggling to eat porridge from a big bowl, before hurrying back to Storna.

Even when Laki was right in front of her, Bokka didn't look up.

"What do you want to do?" Laki asked.

Bokka didn't respond.

Laki squatted down beside her, taking care not to be too close. She didn't say anything else. She couldn't directly counter whatever Pru had been saying. She felt sure it wasn't true, or was misleading in some way, but she hadn't heard the details. She wanted to comfort Bokka, but more importantly, she wanted Bokka to be able to make her own decisions.

"It doesn't matter what I want to do," Bokka said eventually. "Don't let me keep you from your food."

"It can wait, I'm not that hungry," Laki said. "I want to make sure you're okay first."

"Why?" Bokka looked up then, glanced across Laki's face and around the circle. Laki noticed that Bokka had tears in her eyes.

Laki shrugged, not sure how much of a declaration to make in that moment. Would saying too much be as off–putting for Bokka as not saying enough about her feelings? Laki settled on, "Because I like you. I like you, and I saw Pru talking to you, and it seemed like whatever she said was upsetting. So I wanted to come and check with you whether you were okay."

"And when you came, she left." Bokka's voice was sad.

"Which made me think I was right – she was trying to upset you."

"Do you think so?"

"Don't you?"

Bokka moved her shoulders, not so much shrugging as curling into herself. She lifted her knees to her chest and wrapped her arms around them. Laki was briefly distracted by the way this made Bokka's leggings tighten around her thighs. "What Pru said to me... it sounded true. She might have wanted it to upset me, but she was right as well."

The next question felt risky, but Laki couldn't see a way to carry on without knowing. "What did she say?"

"The usual. That I'm not wanted here, that people aren't interested in stone balls, that the things I make aren't useful or beautiful, that I'm not doing enough to help..." Bokka sniffed.

"Well, I don't think that can be true."

"What do you know? You don't have to live here with me, and them, and find out how useless I am. You'll be going back to your lovely Otter Village where everyone is nice to each other and the sun shines all the time." Abandoning her food, Bokka stood up and walked away before Laki could even start to work out how to answer that. Watching Bokka go, she wanted to tell the other woman all the amazing things she had seen. How impressed she was with Bokka's crab catching skills. How splendid she thought the half–finished stone ball would be. How she admired Bokka's commitment to helping Aiso make enough flour.

Bokka had left, though. A few people looked around after her, and Laki knew that if she followed now, the whole thing would be the talk of the village for ages.

That might not be so bad, but Laki wanted some say in how it happened. She went back to sit next to Heln.

"Being bullied?" ey summarised. It had the tone of a question but was simply a fact.

"Being told she's not wanted," Laki added. "Heln..."

"Sal told me that you talked to him about Bokka coming with us," Heln said before she could carry on speaking. Ey pitched eir voice low and leaned close to her ear so that ey couldn't be overheard. "He has doubts, and we'd need to check with her, of course, and her parents and Genu probably, but if she wants to come, I'm willing. We won't be stopping in many places with the rams to get home."

"Won't it be crowded?"

"Yes, but we've traded away a lot of the heavy stuff. The grain is all gone and most of the stone tools. I've seen six people on the boat before, and Aleuks managed well enough with that. Five and two sheep should be possible."

Reassured, Laki said, "I'll ask her as soon as I can. And if she wants to come?"

"She leaves with us.'

"Did Sal tell you...?" It wasn't the place or the time, but if Heln found out about the thefts later, this plan could make Bokka's life worse rather than better.

"That she's not perfect? None of us are." Heln gave Laki a grin which suggested that ey had been involved in some youthful trouble or other, and whether ey had all the details or not, Laki decided ey would cope with and forgive Bokka's exploits.

"Then I'll ask her."

Heln turned away as someone came up behind em and tapped em on eir shoulder.

Laki picked up her bowl of food, now cool, and ate a few more bites. She could go to Klamro and Nerto and Bokka's house as soon as the meal was finished. She could say she had left something there if anyone asked, and hopefully she would have a chance to speak to Bokka alone, properly alone. Or at least perhaps Bokka's parents would be supportive. Surely they would want what was best for their daughter? Maybe they would want her to stay. Maybe they wouldn't accept the truth about how badly she was being treated. This seemed to have been going on for some time, and surely someone could have done something?

Chewing cold meat, Laki watched the crowd laughing and relaxing. Someone started singing. Nobody seemed to have noticed that Bokka was gone – and Nerto and Klamro were still there, talking to Genu. They didn't care, Laki concluded. She would go to ask Bokka straightaway and make things better.

Chapter 8

"BOKKA?" LAKI CALLED AS SHE APPROACHED the door. The village was almost empty – she'd passed one father rocking a young baby to sleep, but most people were still at the communal cooking fire.

"Laki?" Bokka opened the door. "What are you doing here?"

"I came to talk to you." No point trying to disguise a sheep as a stag. "Can I come in? I need to ask you something and you might not want other people to hear, at least not until you've decided the answer."

"Oh." Bokka looked puzzled, but she stepped back from the doorway and let Laki into the round house. The fire was only embers and there was hardly enough light to see each other. Despite this, Laki closed the door behind her. The wood knocked against the stone door post.

Inside the house, there was quiet. Laki could hear Bokka breathing. As her eyes adjusted to the low light, she made out the bed-boxes, the shelves with their food jars and eating bowls, and a little more of Bokka's tearful and frightened expression.

"Are you okay?"

"Fine," Bokka said. "Please... ask what you need to ask."

It wasn't the warm welcome Laki had imagined when she'd pictured this scene, but it would have to do. "I wanted to ask whether you're happy here. And whether you'd like to try being somewhere else for a bit. Whether you'd like to come with us. We're leaving soon – probably loading the boat tomorrow and leaving the day after – and we'll go back to Otter Village by the quickest route, to take the rams home. You could come with us."

Her words weren't as smoothly polished as she'd wanted them to be, either. Bokka's eyes gleamed in the firelight, but she was looking away and Laki couldn't read her expression. "You're asking... if I want to leave?"

"If you want to come with us," Laki repeated.

She heard Bokka sigh.

"You can think about it for a bit." She wanted an answer then and there – she wanted Bokka to say yes, to accept the offer and to choose to spend time with Laki, to choose Laki's village and Laki's company over all the pain of Cow Village. It wouldn't be only one journey, either, not merely a visit to Otter Village for a few weeks, but the rest of their lives together. It was too much to put on this moment and this conversation, so she pushed the idea away. It would return when she woke in the middle of the night, like a deer, scared off once by hunters, coming to drink again at the same river.

"Why are you asking me?" Bokka asked. "Isn't there someone better to go with you?"

For a moment, Laki was confused. She hadn't even considered the possibility that someone else would come with them. "Is there someone else who wants to leave?" she asked. Then she realised that Bokka hadn't understood why Laki was here, specifically. "No, I mean, it's not that we want someone from Cow Village to come with us. I mean, we do, but not just anyone. I'm asking you because I've seen the way Pru and some of the others treat you here. I'm asking you because I can see that you're not happy here. I'm asking you because..." Laki hesitated, because this last reason took them up an entirely different hill, but they'd gone there in their conversation on the clifftop. She stood up straight and went for it. "When we went crabbing, and when we talked afterwards, you said you wanted my necklace and my fur because they'd touched me. Would you like to touch me? Because I'd like to touch you. And if you come with me, if we're away from this village, we'd have more time to explore that."

"So is this a rescue or an invitation?"

"It's an option," Laki said. "I want to offer you the choice, while I'm here, while there is a choice. You know better than me what your other options are. But I came to ask whether you'd like to leave with us because if I didn't ask, you might not even know it was possible."

Bokka turned away then, and bent over what Laki guessed was her own bed. When she straightened up, she was holding a half–made stone ball, six knobs outlined but only two fully carved. She turned it in her hand. "I don't know what to say." Her fingers fitted into the space between those two knobs, and she rubbed it back and forth. She would use a similar movement, Laki thought, when she pecked out the remaining shapes. "What would actually happen? What would I have to do? What's involved?"

"In the journey?"

"In everything."

"Well..." Laki thought. "Can we sit? There are a lot of stages."

"Oh." Bokka moved back and sat on the edge of her bed–box. Laki found a space by the hearth where she had seen Klamro sit when she visited before. It had the advantage that she was facing Bokka, with the fire between them.

"And shall I feed the fire?"

"If you like."

With a poke, and some wood from the nearby pile, and a breath blown in the right place, the embers flared to life again. It seemed very bright after the dimness. Laki was pleased to be able to see Bokka better, although she sensed that Bokka would have been okay in the dark.

"Okay, so, what happens if you say yes?" Laki began, and Bokka nodded along. "First we have to let people know. You probably have to ask your parents, and maybe Genu."

"They'll have to have a village meeting," Bokka said. Her grim tone didn't go with Laki's experience of village meetings.

"I suppose so," Laki said. She thought her doubt showed in her voice, but Bokka only nodded again. "Then, we'll load up the boat, and row away. We might be able to use the sail some of the time. We'll go round the islands and spend most of the day on the water. We'll stop in the evening and make a camp somewhere. We probably won't go into any villages because we've already visited the ones on this coast and we're taking goods home now rather than looking for more trades, but we might meet some people along the way. It'll take us three or four days to reach Otter Village if the weather is good."

"And when we get there?"

"We'll introduce you to everyone in the village. We'll show you round the houses, which are a lot like the ones here except they aren't covered over, each one stands on its own. We'll be guests in someone's house to start with, until we can settle into somewhere. The work to do is all the same, so you'll be able to help me with grinding the flour, and go down to the shore for crabs and limpets, and take the sheep out to graze, and weed the wheat fields, and all the usual things." As she spoke, Laki watched Bokka's face in the firelight. Bokka's eyes were half closed, so perhaps she was imagining the other village, or growing some question which Laki hadn't yet answered.

"So," Bokka began, after a pause. "In Otter Village, I would be..." She broke off again as the door opened. It was Klamro, blinking as ey adjusted to the low light. Laki stood up. Ey came in, with Nerto following close behind.

"Hello, Laki," Klamro said. "I didn't know you were visiting."

"Sorry, I came to..."

"No need to apologise," Nerto said quickly. "You're always welcome here."

"Thank you. I just came to..."

"She came to ask me a question," Bokka cut in. "The answer is yes, Laki."

Laki nodded. "So, as we discussed?"

"I'll ask," Bokka said. "You should go and rest. It'll be a busy few days for you."

*

She didn't always like looking at people's faces, but Bokka enjoyed watching Laki's mouth turn into a smile. Laki gave her a big smile and held it for a moment before turning to leave. "You know where to find me if you need anything."

Bokka did – not that it would be easy to go to Pru and Genu's house, but it might have to be done.

"What's all this about?" Klamro was asking.

Deep breath. Bokka gestured for her parents to sit down and tried to get her thoughts in order.

"I'll have to pack my furs," she said. "It might be cold."

"Pack them for what?" Nerto asked. "It is cold at night, still, but where are you going?"

"To Otter Village."

Nerto had curled into eir bed and now wriggled around to be able to sit up and look at Bokka more clearly. "Is that what Laki was asking you?"

"Yes, to go with them."

"Okay," Klamro said. "Let's get this in order. Laki has asked you to go with the traders when they leave – when are they leaving?"

"Soon. The day after tomorrow, I think."

"And to go with them so that...?"

"So that I can visit Otter Village and live with Laki there."

There was a pause and Bokka saw Nerto's head move. Ey and Klamro were probably communicating in that invisible way of theirs. "Live with Laki there for how long?" Klamro asked.

Bokka didn't know, so she didn't say anything.

"Bokka, how long do you want to stay with Laki?" Nerto's voice was quiet, almost blending in with the crackle of wood from the hearth.

She still didn't have an answer.

"Is this a visit, or a partnership, or what?" Klamro tried.

Bokka didn't know. She wished Laki had stayed. She wished she could go and get Laki – *if you need anything* – did this count as needing something? She tried to remember what Laki had said earlier.

"It's a choice." It wasn't an answer which fitted neatly into the pattern Klamro had started, but it might work. "It's my choice, to go and see somewhere different. To meet different people. Not to have to..." She stopped, feeling the tears coming and her throat clogging up.

"Not to have to?" Nerto prompted.

Bokka realised that she was still standing up. She folded her knees and knelt by the fire, adding a piece of wood mainly for something to do. "You know," she said, sure that her parents had seen what everyone else had seen. "Not to have to listen to what Pru says all the time. Not to have to be stuck here with people who don't like me. Not to be excluded from all the things Storna and Pru and the others are doing."

"Some people here like you."

"I know." Bokka looked up, knowing that Nerto would appreciate even a moment of eye contact. "I don't mean you. Either of you. Or Aiso. But you know that the others my age don't like me. You know they like to try and make me cry. You know I'm good at making things like axe-heads and stone balls and tools, but nobody here encourages me since my aunt died."

"Yes," Klamro said. Eir voice was soft, and Bokka wondered if ey was sad. "We know. But before we say you can go, we need to know whether you understand what you're getting into. What are you going to do in Otter Village? How long are you going to be there? What will you do if you don't like it? What will you do if people there are horrible to you as well?"

Bokka scowled. "Why would they be horrible to me? It's Pru and them who do it. Nobody else would even think of it!"

Another silence in which Klamro and Nerto's heads moved.

"Sometimes you do things which are difficult for people to understand," Nerto said. Bokka shook her head, rejecting that. Some people could understand – look at Klamro and Nerto who thought they understood everything about her! look at Laki who had understood everything about the necklace taking and hadn't even cried about it! – and so everyone else was not making the effort. "People in Otter Village might find it difficult until they get to know you."

A hot tear rolled down Bokka's cheek. They couldn't really be going to stop her because other people might be wrong as well. "But it's not true," she said and couldn't hold back a sob. "Laki understands! She said what Pru said wasn't true!"

Klamro moved over to kneel next to eir daughter. "Can I hug you?"

Bokka sniffed and nodded. Klamro wrapped a warm arm around her shoulders and she leaned sideways into em.

"I don't know what Pru said," ey told her. "And I'm glad that Laki does understand. And I don't think Nerto or I wants to stop you going – we'd miss you, of course, but we know you're old enough to make your own decisions and have your own adventures. We merely want to make sure you know what you're doing. We've all heard stories about people who ran away and got into worse trouble. I wouldn't want to think that you'd left here because it's difficult to get on with people, only to find it even harder somewhere else, or even that they were treating you badly. What if these traders try to trade you for something else at the next village?"

"They won't," Bokka said. "Laki told me they're going straight back to Otter Village, as fast as they can."

"It's only the beginning of the summer, don't they have more trading to do?"

"Because they got the rams," Bokka assured her parents. "They have to go back as soon as possible."

"You seem very sure about this," Nerto commented from eir place the other side of the fire.

Bokka nodded. "I trust Laki."

"That's good," Klamro said. "Was it her idea? You've never mentioned wanting to leave before."

"I didn't know I could." That was true, but only part of the truth. Bokka added, "I've wanted things to change before now. I've tried to be different myself, and I've tried to explain how I see things, and I've asked people to change how things are..." She knew her parents would remember some of those attempts, at least. "It wasn't working. I haven't tried anything for a while. I didn't think there was anything else to do except keep quiet and focus on grinding wheat and catching crabs and try to stay out of Pru's way. But Laki says there's something else, that people in other places are different, and I want to go and find out for myself."

"Yes, I can see that." Nerto gave a kind of nod.

"You'll need to check with Genu, too," Klamro said.

"And will he make the village have a meeting?"

"Probably, but we'll be there to support you," Nerto said. "And they can't actually stop you leaving, even if you and the traders have to go at night or something. You'd better get some sleep now, and tomorrow we'll pack the things you'll need. You'd better have your winter cloak, and we can bake double bread so you've some to take with you, and..."

Bokka stopped listening. They were saying yes. She was going to go. She was going to leave Cow Village, with Laki, and go to Otter Village. She was going to sail in Heln's splendid boat. She was going to see new places. She was going to meet new people.

"I won't have time to finish the ball," she said suddenly. From the way Nerto's head jerked, Bokka thought she'd probably interrupted, but it was too late. "I haven't finished carving it." She took the stone ball with its two out of six finished knobs out of her pouch and held it up.

"You can take it with you," Nerto said. "I'm sure they have stone carving in Otter Village. You might even be able to work on it on the way, if there are quiet times. And having it with you will help you stay calm when things are strange."

"Okay." Bokka lay back on her bed and stroked the curves of it. "Okay, and I'll bring it back one day when it's finished."

"You do that," Klamro said. Ey sounded sad for some reason. Bokka fell asleep thinking of spending time with Laki and the things they would make together.

*

As Bokka had feared, Genu made the whole village meet to discuss whether or not she could go. To her surprise, the traders came, too. Laki sat right by her side, and Heln, Marko, and Sal all sat behind them. It was meant to be a quick meeting before they went on with their work, and the weather was good, so a crowd had gathered at the entrance to the village in an area which had been paved to stop it getting too muddy in the winter.

"We have to sense whether this is really what Goddess requires," Genu said ominously as he opened the meeting. "Bokka's parents have agreed to manage without her for the summer season, but every single member of the village should have a say."

That wasn't going to happen, because a good number of people had already decided that the meeting wasn't a good use of their time. Even from where they had gathered, Bokka could see Aiso's son grinding wheat – he was being over–aggressive and spilling half the flour out the sides of the quern before he could gather it into his bowl. Pru had given an excuse for Storna, who was walking down to the beach to collect driftwood and bone and whatever else had come in on last night's tide. And most of the children who were old enough to be useful had been sent to check on the cattle and the sheep. Nevertheless, there were enough people there to make her life uncomfortable, and Pru was bound to want to try and stop her from leaving.

There was a short silence, in which Genu stayed standing and visibly fidgeted.

Aiso waved his hand. He didn't stand, and Bokka guessed that his knees were sore again. Genu ignored him, ostentatiously looking around to see if anyone else wanted to speak, before eventually calling Aiso.

"I think our young people should be free to come and go as they choose," he said. "I think Bokka should see other villages if she wants to, but I don't think this is just about her. Let's have it understood that people can visit, and come, and go. I did when I was her age, and getting to know how things are done in other villages did me the world of good. I still came back to my home village in the end."

"I see, I see," Genu said as Aiso finished. "Anyone else? What do we think?"

Pru stood up and Genu nodded approvingly.

"Well," Pru began, "I'm not sure about this, but overall, I think Bokka should probably stay. We'd miss her help with the flour–making. It would certainly take at least one more person at the grindstones to replace the work she does there. Someone else might have to sit around for days making little stone balls with bumps on, because I'm sure we need those. And nobody else can be bothered to pick up limpets like she does."

Bokka flushed hot, then cold, as Pru was speaking. At first, she was angry because she thought Pru was really going to try and make her stay. Then she realised that Pru didn't mean any of it, that her reasons for wanting Bokka to stay were actually comments on how useless Bokka was and why she should go. By the time Pru folded herself elegantly down again, Bokka was confused and wanted to stay and prove how useful she was and leave and never see Pru again and probably something else as well.

Laki touched the back of her hand. It was a gentle stroke, not a rough touch. It startled Bokka at first, but as Laki let her fingers rest there, quietly, while Genu was saying something else, Bokka found that it was reassuring.

Genu paused. Nobody else was standing to speak. "Are there no further comments?" he asked. "At the moment we have one for and one against. We need to hear from someone else in order to decide this."

Laki shifted slightly. Bokka wondered if she was going to say something. She did – but not by standing. Instead, she leaned over to whisper in Bokka's ear, "You could give your own view."

Bokka frowned, remembering to turn her head so that Laki could see it. "No," she whispered back. "Not allowed!" She didn't know why Laki would even suggest it – didn't they have village meetings in Otter Village?

More movement. Bokka looked down at the ground, wishing the sea would rise so far about the tide line it would come and cover her. Next to her, Laki seemed to have looked around, and then stood.

"Laki," Genu said, "this is a surprise. I'm not even sure whether strangers are allowed to speak in the village meeting."

"Anyone present might be called by Goddess to speak," Laki said. She spoke firmly in a way which made Bokka think she had been taught that by someone authoritative. "I want to share some of the reasons why I invited Bokka to travel with us."

"Okay," Genu said, although he barely had time before Laki continue anyway.

"It's important for us to learn from other people," Laki said. "I've learned so much on this trading trip, visiting other villages. I've learned so much from you and your hospitality, from the wonderful people here in Cow Village." Bokka hadn't thought that Laki liked the people here at all, so that was a strange thing to say. "I want Bokka to have the same opportunity. Even a short visit to Otter Village will give her a chance to meet new people, to learn about our tomb, to see how we tend our sheep and shape our fields –" Both jobs Bokka didn't think were the slightest bit interesting. What was Laki talking about? "– and to learn new skills. I'm going back to Otter Village much more experienced than I left, and I'll be much more useful to them as a result. Won't that benefit you in the long run, even if you miss her this summer?" Laki hadn't said anything before about Bokka having to come back. So, this invitation was only temporary. Maybe she didn't really want to go at all – it would be that much harder to tolerate Pru's bullying after a few moons of freedom from it.

Other people were standing up now. Laki was sitting by Bokka again, and she must have noticed that Bokka was upset, because she put a hand on Bokka's shoulder. It wasn't enough to really explain what was happening. It did help Bokka take a deep breath and decide to trust Laki until she could ask for an explanation later.

"If it's so great, I ought to be allowed to go," Pru was saying. Bokka shivered.

"We only have room for one extra in the boat, with the two rams as well," Heln answered.

"So why her?" Pru added a sob, which Bokka assumed was a fake one, for effect.

"Because Laki invited her." Heln's voice was steady. "Laki invited her, and I supported that invitation."

The meeting turned into an uproar. Bokka covered her ears, no longer able to pick out the individual voices.

Chapter 9

THE REST OF THE DAY WAS ALL about packing. Laki seemed to have her things done in less time than it took Bokka to walk back from the disastrous meeting to the house. "Do you want me to help?" Laki asked, but Bokka shook her head.

"Klamro will help me." Not that it wouldn't have been nice to spend some time with Laki, but Klamro knew her things better, and they had a pattern for packing for overnight hunting trips. It would be easier. And Laki was angry about the way the meeting had been held. She had said so to Bokka, who had shrugged and said it was always like that. Laki had then whispered to Heln for some time, only to be met with another shrug. "People do things differently," ey said.

"But Goddess needs to be able to speak!" Laki had been vehement, but Bokka didn't care, so long as the result was that she was allowed to go.

"Good." Laki nodded now. "When you're done, come down to the beach and find us. We'll be checking the boat and maybe loading some things, ready for the morning. Heln has been watching the tide and ey says conditions will be best immediately before dawn. I could wish it was just after dawn, but you know how it is!"

Bokka was not sure that she knew, but she nodded anyway and went to pack. Some things, like her clothes, were obvious. Other things, like the collection of antler and bone tools she used for very specialised stone working, she felt she wanted to take but Klamro thought she was unlikely to need. They ended up arguing, Bokka's chest tight with the fear of what was to come. She couldn't find a way to say it, though. She simply tried to pack as many of her things as she could carry, ending up with a heavy and bulging leather bag and a favourite sleeping fur which she could wrap around her.

*

That night, Marko and Heln didn't come into the village to sleep. They stayed on the grassy strip at the top of the beach, where people often cooked or sat to knap flints or make pots, and took turns to rest. "I don't want to miss the moment and have to wait until the afternoon tide," Heln explained when Laki asked why ey couldn't sleep indoors.

"Won't you be tired?"

"Not that tired – I have Marko to share it with," Heln said. "And when it comes to the sailing, I'll have Sal and you and Bokka as well to share it with."

Laki ate with Bokka's family, although she had to go back to Genu and Pru's house to sleep. She actually wasn't sure why, but Nerto and Klamro were quite clear about it, and Laki guessed they might want a chance to speak to Bokka alone before she left.

As planned, it was still dark when Sal knocked on the door of Genu's house and called softly for Laki. She had hoped that Genu at least, and perhaps Pru, would sleep through it. No such luck. Indeed, the whole village seemed to have gathered in the cool grey half–light as Laki waded out to the boat, loaded her bag, and put Bokka's in, too.

Bokka explained that she had never had to climb into a boat from the water before – Cow Village had never replaced the boat lost in a storm, and so she hadn't had the chance – and so Laki helped her. Bokka looked embarrassed, but Laki gave her a big grin anyway. It hadn't been a hardship at all to hold Bokka's firmly muscled and bare leg to give her a hand up into the boat.

"Remember us!" Pru called tearfully from the shore as they put their oars into the water. Laki thought that Pru's excessive display of emotion was holding some of the others back; certainly, there were no other shouts and only some small gestures of farewell as they went.

"Perfect timing," Heln said, as the falling tide helped them out of the bay and round the cliffs with minimal effort. Even the wind was right. The sun rose as they headed south, staying in sight of the shore but far enough out to miss the rocks in the shallow water, and with the whole day ahead of them, Heln predicted they would make good progress. Laki and Sal rowed as Heln steered and encouraged, "That's it, keep going."

In Laki's fantasies, once they were out of Cow Village and on the boat, everything would be okay. Bokka would smile and laugh, and they'd talk, and sit together, and perhaps hug and kiss... she'd fallen asleep imagining that.

In reality, she could see Bokka, but they couldn't talk. To balance the boat, Laki and Sal sat in the middle to paddle. Heln sat behind them with a third paddle which ey could use to steer.

Bokka and Marko were right at the front of the boat. There wasn't much space up there, not least because the rams were also travelling at the front. The sheep had their legs tied to prevent them running away, but they wriggled determinedly now and then, enough to feel the rocking and vibrations through the planks of the boat. Marko ignored the sheep and gazed out at the shoreline as it passed them and pointed out dolphins now and again. Bokka kept a wary eye on the wriggly sheep. Laki thought she was probably anxious about one of them escaping and knocking her overboard.

At first, paddling the boat took most of Laki's attention. The movement, the balance, the need to match Sal's stokes... but with time the rhythm came back to them. Laki and Sal had taken turns with Marko and Heln all the way to Cow Village. Although they had taken the journey more slowly and stopped in at several villages on the way, they'd covered the same distance and established their patterns. After a while, Heln didn't need to give more instructions. Their course was set, and they were making good progress.

"Everything okay at the bow?" Heln asked.

"Seems fine," Marko told em. "Sheep are settling down."

"We'll stop for a break, feed and water them, when the sun is a bit higher."

Laki saw Marko scan the shore, checking the state of the tide against the rocks, perhaps looking to see where fresh water ran down to the sea and where there might be a bay or a beach for a short rest. "Let me know when you're ready. I'm watching for good places."

Then Laki's paddle went in at an awkward angle and jarred her arm and she had to give her full attention to the boat for a while.

*

By the time they stopped for a break, Bokka was starting to relax into the sensations of being at sea. The rocking of the boat had been frightening at first, but as she realised that it wasn't dangerous – that the others were fine about it, and that it didn't mean the thing was about to tip over – she started to enjoy it. It was soothing, if you let it happen. She kept a close eye on the rams, too. The two of them were next to each other, in the bottom of the boat, with their feet tied and their backs leaning on each other. Their eyes were round and wild as they struggled periodically, although Bokka thought they should know that people being there meant they were safe. Perhaps they were worried about the rocking, as she had been at the beginning.

Stopping meant everything changed again, though. She had to get out of the boat, wading through the seawater to the shore, only to have Heln hand her a rope and ask her to hold the boat while ey unloaded some bowls for fresh water. She had thought they would let the sheep out as well, but Sal simply cut a pile of fodder from the shore and took it out to the boat. He made sure the rams could eat before coming back to join the others on the beach.

Laki offered her some bread and cheese, last–minute trades from Cow Village for things which would last well on their journey.

Bokka almost refused the food. At home, she wouldn't eat a midday meal with others, but usually helped herself to leftovers or found something to snack on wherever she was.

"Best to eat while we're on shore," Laki said, still holding it out.

"And it's your turn to row next," Heln added. "That's hungry work."

Her turn to row? She hoped Heln was ready for something to go wrong, because she'd never rowed before. But she took the bread and cheese from Laki, breaking off some small pieces, and when she ate, she discovered she was already hungry.

Paddling didn't go as badly as she'd feared, either. When they were ready to set off again, Marko sat beside her in the boat and talked through all the steps—how to hold the paddle, how to dip it into the water and when to pull on it. Marko made it sound not too difficult, but not like something she should already have known. She'd started to feel embarrassed, with Laki watching her from the bow, that she didn't already paddle like an expert. Surely in Otter Village they learned as babies and Laki would think her childish for never having done this before? But Marko behaved as if it was perfectly normal to learn a new skill as an adult, and answered her questions patiently, and adjusted his speed to match the length of her strokes.

Bokka pulled hard. She watched her paddle move through the water, and come up dripping, and go back. Once she had the pattern, it was soothing, like the waves lapping the shore, or pecking circles into her stone ball.

"We're making good progress," Heln said. Laki chose a beach for them, and they stopped as the sun was setting behind them.

By the time she was standing above the high–tide line, with the boat pulled up behind her and Sal starting a cooking fire in front of her, Bokka felt that she was ready to simply fall forwards and go to sleep, regardless of her hunger and the lack of shelter. Standing upright took all her strength, and she didn't know what else to do.

"Here," Laki said, coming up beside Bokka. Laki bumped Bokka's overnight bag gently against her hand – Klamro had helped her pack the things she would need to sleep out for a night. Klamro was still in Cow Village and so was Nerto and only Goddess knew when they would see each other again. Bokka took the bag from Laki with a little nod, but still couldn't work out what to do next.

Moving slowly, and making sure that Bokka saw her moving, Laki put a hand on Bokka's shoulder. "Are you okay?"

Bokka wasn't sure. She didn't want to nod or shake her head, in case Laki thought it was a definite yes or no answer. It was difficult to put words together, so she stayed still until something came. She thought Laki might say something else or move away. Laki didn't – she also stood still until Bokka was able to say, "I don't know. I'm tired."

That was true, she realised when she'd said it. Her arms and legs and shoulders and eyes ached from the paddling and the sun reflecting off the sea and the strangeness of all this.

"Yes," Laki said. She didn't seem as tired as Bokka felt, but perhaps she was more used to these sorts of things. "Come and have something to eat. Sal's making a quick stew with hazelnuts and dried meat, and we've still got plenty of bread."

A gentle pressure on Bokka's shoulder steered her over to the fire and to a place to sit on a convenient rock. Laki sat beside her with no discussion. *Perhaps that is the good thing about being in a small group,* Bokka thought. There were only five of them and nobody wanted to make her feel horrible. In fact, only Laki was paying her any attention at all. Sal was busy with the food, and Heln and Marko had gone into the edge of the woods with the sheep. They would find a bush the sheep could graze on and tie them up there for a while.

"What do you think of the boat?" Laki asked. "My first day on the sea, when we were trying it out before we set off on this trading voyage, it was rougher than it has been today, and it made me feel queasy. I got used to it the next day. But you seem to have been fine."

She hadn't felt sick, it was true, although maybe the way her stomach said it wasn't hungry even when it was empty was something related. "Yes, I'm fine. It's hard work, though. I don't know how you did that all morning and didn't fall asleep when we stopped at midday. I ache all over." Bokka rubbed her upper arm with her opposite hand to demonstrate the pain. Laki echoed the gesture, rubbing Bokka's other arm.

It felt good. The skin was covered by the top of her tunic, but it was still Laki touching her. Bokka turned towards Laki, looking at her necklace where it rested over her collarbones. "And my shoulders." Bokka raised her left hand from her right upper arm to her right shoulder, and luckily Laki copied her, raising her hand from Bokka's upper left arm to her left shoulder. "There." Bokka sighed as Laki rubbed the sore muscles with firm fingers.

"Food's hot, doves," Sal said. "Come and eat some before you get too distracted."

Laki snorted, which was confusing, and took her hand away from Bokka, which was cold. She stood up. Bokka copied reluctantly, her legs preferring not to do anymore work. "Doves?" she asked Laki.

"You know how rock doves coo at each other and rub their necks together?" Laki asked. Bokka nodded, picturing the soft grey feathers of them and how a well–aimed slingshot stone could take one down for a good meal. "Sal's saying we're being like that."

They hadn't rubbed their necks together, only put hands on each other... but now that she pictured copying the doves, Bokka could see the appeal. That soft skin on Laki's neck—being that close to her—sounded good. But Laki was already moving away, towards the fire and food. Bokka followed.

The best that could be said for the food was that it was food. There hadn't been time to collect anything fresh. The stew was made with a dried meat which Bokka found too salty. The cold bread was okay but a bit dry. Between the dryness and the salt, Bokka had to go and refill a bowl with fresh water from the stream to drink. She stopped eating before the others were finished.

"Have you had enough?" Laki asked. "There's plenty, don't worry about saving it for tomorrow."

That hadn't even occurred to Bokka. She nodded. She could have eaten more, if it had been nice, but she was no longer hungry, so what she had eaten probably counted as "enough."

When the meal was finished, they repacked things in the boat – not carried ashore this time, but anchored in the bay. Heln explained that it was easier for a single night's stay, and that someone would keep watch in case the tide or strong winds pulled the boat away.

"Or a wolf comes for the sheep," Bokka added.

"More likely to try for our leftover cooked food," Sal said. He and Marko had settled the rams on ropes pegged into the ground so they could move about and graze but not wander off.

The last light was going from the sky, Bokka noticed, as she watched the others fetching furs from their bags and settling down to sleep. She wasn't sure where to go. Apart from a couple of hunting trips, where Nerto had pitched a leather tent for them to shelter under, Bokka had always slept in the stone safety of her bed–box. Heln and Marko lay next to each other, close to the fire. Sal wrapped his fur around his shoulders and went to sit by the high–tide line, out of the glare of the fire where his eyes could adjust to the dark to take the first turn at watching. Laki spread her fur by the other side of the fire, then beckoned to Bokka.

"Here, you can sleep next to me," she said.

"I'm worried I won't be able to sleep at all."

"I can hug you to keep you warm if it's cold." Laki was smiling. It was a nice thought—Bokka would like a hug from Laki—but it was as likely to keep her awake as help her sleep.

"I mean, with nothing over us. Won't all the stars bother you? On our long hunting trips from Cow Village we always have a tent."

"It'll be fine," Laki said. "Not a cloud in the sky, and it's warm. We'll be covered in our furs. There might be a bit of dew, or some mist in the morning, but nothing to worry about. How would the stars bother us?"

"Just... so many, so bright," Bokka said, but she could tell that Laki wouldn't be bothered at all. She knew there was a tent in the boat in case of rain, but she didn't want to make a fuss and make Laki and the others think that she was scared. And she couldn't really go out into the water on her own to fetch it, especially because she didn't know where in the boat they'd stored it. She lay down next to Laki, wrapping her fur all the way around her and rolling to face her. The ground was firm, but the grass went some way to cushioning it.

"There, you've got the fire behind you," Laki said. "That'll keep you warm."

They were speaking in soft voices. Bokka could hear Marko whispering something to Heln, but she couldn't make out the words, so she hoped the same would apply the other way around. "I'm not cold," she said. "But you've mentioned it twice. Are you warm enough?"

"You're blocking the fire's heat from reaching me," Laki pointed out. Bokka made a face and started to move—she didn't want Laki to be cold—but Laki reached out a hand to stop her. "You can stay there," Laki said. "It's fine. But perhaps you could hug me to keep me warm?"

The thought make Bokka feel warm before they were even touching. She could feel her face heating up. "I could." She reached out and Laki wriggled closer, first overlapping the edges of their furs and then wrapping an arm around Bokka. Bokka mirrored the movement until they were face to face, breasts to breasts, belly to belly. And arm to arm – their lower arms were trapped between them.

"Under your head," Laki murmured, shifting back far enough to move her lower arm upwards. It took Bokka a moment to imagine what would happen, but when she did, she lifted her head, let Laki's arm under, and was soon resting on the pillow of Laki's upper arm. She couldn't quite copy the movement, because Laki's shoulder would be in the way. In any case, Laki had already made herself a little makeshift pillow from a rolled leather cloak.

"It's okay," Laki said when she realised what Bokka was looking at. "Come back close and keep me warm."

Neither of them had undressed, just slipped their belts off so that they were only wearing tunics and knee–length leg–coverings, suitable for wading in and out of the sea. Laki's tunic had deep slits in the side, where the front and back hadn't been sown together, making it easier for her to move and squat during the day. This also meant, Bokka realised, that it fell down at night and left some skin exposed over Laki's hip. Laki had asked to be hugged. Bokka's hand explored, up and down Laki's back, over the end of the tunic and... Bokka almost gasped as she touched the amazing softness and warmth of Laki's bare skin for the first time.

"Not too far," Laki whispered as she pressed closer. "We do need to sleep."

Bokka wasn't sure what would count as "too far" so she stopped moving her hand. Perhaps Laki thought that she'd been trying to initiate sex, which wasn't her intention; only to touch... "Are you comfortable like that?" she asked.

Laki nodded, a gesture Bokka felt more than saw as the curls of Laki's hair brushed over her cheek. She liked being close to Laki. It was even better than having Laki's necklace to hold or Laki's fur to keep her warm. Focussing on the sensation, any worries Bokka had about the next day faded away and she fell asleep quickly.

*

The journey seemed to Laki to have taken almost no time. Compared with the slow pace at which they'd travelled away from Otter Village, they'd positively raced back. As the coast turned east and Laki began to recognise landmarks – places she had walked to in her childhood, places she'd stopped to fish a year ago – she got more and more excited for home.

"Everyone will welcome us," she told Bokka. "We'll land the boat on the beach and unload. We'll take the rams up the path and put them into a little space fenced with hurdles to recover for a day or two before we introduce them to the flock. We'll meet lots of friends and find somewhere to stay and have a lovely meal with fresh bread..."

"If there's enough," Heln said. "Remember that we know we're on the way, but they don't. All this will be new to them, and a surprise. I'm sure we will be welcomed. Aleuks knows that I'll come back when the trading is done, and Trebbi is a leader who welcomes guests easily, but they don't know we're arriving today. Everyone might be busy with something else. And things can have changed while we were away. There could have been an illness, or a death, or a crop might have failed. We won't know until we get there."

Laki saw Bokka shiver and tried to soften the impact of Heln's words without denying their truth. "They'll all do what they can to help us, though, whatever else is happening," she said. "We're coming home. We'll be welcome."

"I'm sure," Heln agreed. "And the more welcome, in my experience, for remembering that we are a surprise, and being patient with people."

"I hope my brothers and uncles are all well," Marko said. "And I don't think we need to worry about spaces to sleep; it hasn't been long enough for that many babies to be born, so unless another trading party is visiting, or everyone got fed up with Dog Village and left to stay with us in Otter Village, there will be empty beds for us to fill."

"My family house is probably standing entirely empty," Laki reflected. "With me gone and my mother dead, my father was planning to go and live with his sister."

The speculation, unfounded though it mostly was, passed the time pleasantly. It was a beautiful day, and the sea was almost flat. "The first time I arrived at Otter Village, we almost drowned," Heln remembered as they approached the beach with the midafternoon sun high above them. "Aleuks and I were managing this boat with two of us—you can see it's a bit too big for that—because we'd lost another crew member to a storm not long before.

Trebbi had to swim out to help us bring the boat in. Much easier to find the bay today!"

Marko pulled an exaggerated anxious face. "I hadn't even met you then. I'm glad Trebbi and Dru were there to help you."

And it had meant that people in the village knew as soon as they arrived, Laki realised when they'd pulled the boat up the beach and nobody else had appeared. "Did they not see us?" she asked.

"Probably not," Heln agreed. "You can't really see the shore from the village, and they're probably busy with other things. Why don't you run up and find someone? Word will spread soon enough."

"Bokka, would you like to come, too?" Laki was keen to show Bokka the way, although Bokka herself looked shocked, with wide eyes and a blank expression. When Bokka shrugged, Laki took that as enough agreement and took her hand. "Come on, I'll show you the way. We won't be long!" she called to Heln and the others.

The path up to the village hadn't changed much. It was a little overgrown, as many paths were in the summer, with long grasses and flowers taking over the space. Laki noted a thick patch of dandelions; their leaves were young, and she might come back to pick some later. As they walked, she pointed out what they could see, trying to help Bokka get orientated quickly. "You can see the trees up there, on the edge of the cliff; the tomb is right past there. But the village is this way, all our houses are near the fields, and there are some pens for the animals."

As they turned the corner and the houses were in sight, so were some people. "Trebbi!" Laki called at once. "Dru! Aleuks!" Everyone dropped what they were doing and came rushing over.

Chapter 10

BOKKA HAD NEVER MET SO MANY new people in one go. She had thought that market days with a couple of the nearby villages were busy days, with crowds and too much noise, but those were only a selected handful of adults from each place. When you go to whole new village, there aren't only some traders and some storytellers. There are people and more people and families and children and an old man who thinks it's a good idea to welcome you with a hug without asking first and everyone tells you their name but by the time you've turned round you have no idea which name goes with which person.

"Are you hungry?" Laki asked at some point, and Bokka could only nod. At least if she was eating people probably wouldn't expect her to talk, and she couldn't call someone by the wrong name and upset them.

Laki brought her a chunk of freshly baked bread—it was delicious after the bread they'd eaten on the way, cold and getting drier every day—and reassuringly similar to the bread she ate at home. Laki also brought a bowl of stew, but it had been made with different herbs to the ones they used in Cow Village and Bokka found it difficult to eat.

"What do you want?" Laki asked later.

"Hmm?"

"Come with me." Away from the gathering, at the edge of a field of wheat, Laki asked again. "What do you want to do now? You were being very quiet there, and it's been a long day, so I thought... do you need sleep? Something else to eat? Something else?"

"Rest," Bokka said. She already felt better, away from the noise of so many excited voices, but a bit more quiet would be even better. "I don't suppose..." She didn't know how to ask; earlier, Laki had shown her the house with the spare beds, the two bed-boxes so similar to the ones at home and yet different because Laki would be in the one next to hers. But she didn't want to get into a stone–built box yet. She would sleep later. Now, she wanted to be close to Laki, the way they had slept close together wrapped in their furs on the beach.

Perhaps Laki had read her mind, though, or something in the way she stood or moved suggested her thoughts, because Laki stepped towards her so that their shoulders almost touched. "Suppose what?"

"That you—that we could—" Laki was close enough to touch. Bokka wondered whether it was a good idea—that old man who hugged without permission?—but Laki had come close and could move away if she wanted to. Bokka reached out.

Laki moved, too, and they were hugging. Bokka ran her hand up and down Laki's back, stroking. Laki copied the movement. It was very soothing. Bokka pressed her face into Laki's shoulder for a moment, before thinking of something else she would like to do.

"Kiss?" Laki asked, as Bokka turned her face up towards Laki's. Like two birds in a flock, they moved together, not exactly the same path but in the same pattern...

Kissing was good. Bokka had experimented with a boy from Ewe Village who had visited one day when it rained and they'd hidden under a huge old oak tree, but that had been two years ago. She couldn't even remember his name. It had felt good, but it hadn't been anything like this. Laki went on moving one hand up and down Bokka's back, pulling her close, keeping her close, while her other hand rested on Bokka's shoulder. Bokka wasn't sure where her own hands were anymore. Her whole attention had narrowed to her lips.

Laki pulled back for long enough to take a deep breath. Bokka moaned a noise of frustration, found one of her hands, and put it along Laki's cheek to tug her slowly back into the kiss. They deepened it. Bokka explored Laki's lips with her tongue. Laki's hand rested on her lower back and their hips pushed together. Bokka found herself full of longings for touches she could hardly imagine or name.

Neither of them tried to move beyond kissing for the moment, though. Bokka realised that she was actually standing very still, only her mouth and head moving as Laki took a turn licking into the corners of Bokka's lips. She might have expected Laki to taste of bread, or stew, or the yarrow that people here apparently liked to cook with. Instead, Laki tasted sweet, perhaps a little of the sea (saltwater still on her skin?) and of the wood smoke from the fire.

Bokka was starting to wonder if they would ever stop—if they would ever have to stop, now that she was breathing through her nose while they kissed—when there was a soft sound behind Laki and they both jerked to look up and around.

"Don't worry about me," Trebbi said with a smile. She was walking past, and Bokka didn't know enough about the village to know where she would be going or why. "But now I know why you wanted to take that little old house for just the two of you. Be patient. The roof needs replacing. But we'll do it later this summer and if you decide to stay, you may well be in there for the winter."

"Thanks, Trebbi." Laki nodded to the older woman but then turned, very deliberately, back to face Bokka. Trebbi went on her way and Laki tried to resume the kiss.

Enjoyable though it had been, Bokka now had something else on her mind. "If we decide to stay? She's serious?"

"I told you people here would welcome you," Laki said. Even though she was saying "I told you so," she was smiling, so Bokka thought she wasn't too upset about not being believed. "And although I didn't know that house was still empty—or even still standing, it's been in need of some repairs for a while—I knew Trebbi and Aleuks would try and find us somewhere to live if we want to be part of Otter Village."

Bokka let Laki give her a quick kiss, but she had other questions. "Trebbi and Aleuks are partners, right?"

Laki nodded.

"And it's their house we're staying in?"

"Yes." Laki sighed. "I thought we might be able to go to my family's house, like Sal is, and Marko is, or find somewhere on our own, but at least Trebbi doesn't mind having us."

This had been a big discussion earlier in the day. Bokka hadn't followed it then, preferring to go and help with the bread–making. Now she pressed her palm to the back of Laki's neck, tugging her closer for another slow and gentle kiss. "We could sleep outside again if we want to," she said when the kiss finished.

"We could," Laki said, but her voice was very flat. "But it's cold, and damp, and we can sleep indoors and still spend all day tomorrow together."

That was true. Bokka was looking forward to it, although she was worried that when they were given their jobs for the day, they would actually end up separated. What if Laki was sent off to work on the roof or in the fields, and Bokka ended up grinding flour with people she'd never met before? She wished she had something of Laki's to keep close for comfort.

*

Laki woke up the next morning with high hopes for the day. She would see her friends. She would spend time with Bokka. She would help with something – maybe in the fields. And she would talk to Trebbi about roof repairs, and they would make a plan, and she and Bokka would be on their way to living together in their own private space.

Some of these were easily accomplished. As she and Bokka ate together, next to the hearth fire in Trebbi's house, Trebbi came to join them. Laki asked about roof repairs – what would be needed, how long would it take, what could she do to help, what skills were involved?

Trebbi laughed a bit, saying that it couldn't be done alone, and the best time would be the end of the summer, when the harvest was done and the reeds could be cut from the lake side, but she answered all Laki's questions patiently. Laki decided that there were some things which could be started. You needed long straight poles for the supports, for example, and those could be cut and put to dry much earlier in the season.

Other complications arose, however. The first one was easily fixed. When Laki realised that one of the pouches she usually wore on her belt was missing, she mentioned this to Bokka and simply held out her hand until Bokka returned it.

"I'm sorry," Bokka said, several times. "I wanted..."

"To feel near me, yes, I know," Laki said. She put a hand on Bokka's waist so that they were close, face to face, although Bokka was still looking down at her feet. "Bokka, you're going to be near me. We can choose what to do. We can choose to spend all day together if we want to. You don't need to take anything of mine. You've got me."

"And will you choose to do the same things as me?" Bokka asked.

"Of course," Laki said. "I wouldn't go off and leave you with people you've never met, would I?" That seemed genuinely obvious to Laki, and Bokka's shrug, which suggested that plenty of people would do exactly that, both saddened and annoyed her. "Maybe Pru would, I don't know, but I'm not going to. Bokka, I asked you here so we could be together, not to run away from you as soon as we arrived."

As soon as she said that, she wondered if "be together" was too strong – should she have said "spend time together" or something similar? Or maybe she meant "be together," in that full, strong sense, and it was the right thing to say. She did want to. The kissing last night had been amazing, and if Bokka was interested...

Laki found it hard to tell that sometimes. Bokka was interested in being near her, and her things—hence the missing pouch—but also seemed distracted by everything going on around them. Laki decided to give it a few days and see how things developed. There would always be ways to find some time for the two of them to spend alone. That could come after Bokka had settled in a bit.

That first morning, Laki offered to grind wheat for Trebbi and Aleuks. It was a straightforward job, she knew how to do it, she knew Bokka was good at it, too, and she knew Trebbi often struggled to find time, especially when she was being called away to see what was happening all around the village and make decisions about planting, harvesting, and storing food.

"Thank you," Trebbi said. "But don't you want to come and see the rams settled in?" They were outside because Trebbi had already been called to attend to that.

Laki looked at Bokka, who shrugged.

"We'll visit them later," Laki said. "If we spend the morning at the quern stone outside here, everyone in the village will come past at some point, and I'll be able to introduce everyone to Bokka."

"I thought we'd do that all together, at the meeting tomorrow night." Bokka shuddered, and if Laki saw it, Trebbi did, too. "Or not. You're still welcome to come to our meeting, of course. And thanks for helping with the flour. Wheat's in a jar on the shelves, you know how much to do for four of us, and a bit extra if you can. There's usually someone who needs some help."

Bokka went back inside to get the wheat. Aleuks came up the path, saying to Trebbi, "Ready to go?"

"Yes," Trebbi said. "And don't worry about the wheat later, Bokka and Laki are going to take care of it for all of us."

"Excellent." Aleuks gave Laki a grin and a nod, and Laki noticed that she did look similar to Heln—something about the eyes, the jaw. Then Trebbi and Aleuks went on their way, and Laki was alone by the time Bokka returned with the bowl of wheat for grinding.

Laki showed her the quern stone, shared between three houses and on the edge of the main path through the village. "It's a good spot because you'll get to meet everyone who comes by," Laki explained as she started grinding the first handful.

"Is that good?" Bokka asked. Laki wasn't sure whether she was joking and decided to simply answer the question.

"It is if you want to get to know people."

Bokka shrugged and picked a leaf of grass from beside the quern. "I might. But people often don't want to get to know me."

"What do you mean?" Laki could have said more but put her shoulders into the rhythm of the grinding instead. Bokka would answer as fully as she wanted to.

"Well, at home, people don't want to spend time with me," Bokka said. "My parents sometimes. Aiso talks to me while I'm making flour, but only because I'm making his as well. But all the other things I do on my own—I carve my stone spheres, I find crabs and limpets, I might go fishing or search for fruits or roots in the woods. Even if I'm weeding the field, I'm left to do it on my own while the others are chatting or singing in another field. They never let me go swimming with them or anything like that."

"Not everyone is like that," Laki said.

"You're not," Bokka conceded. "But when I meet new people..." She trailed off with a shrug.

"I can see why you'd be worried," Laki agreed. "But I think people here are..." She didn't want to say *nicer* because some of the people in Cow Village who had been horrible to Bokka had been nice to her. "I think you'll find it easier to make friends."

She didn't think Bokka was convinced, but instead of arguing, Bokka fetched a little tool from her pouch and started work on the next knob on her stone ball.

The first person to come past was easy to talk to, because it was Sal. He was going to help with the rams but stopped to chat, asking Laki how she was finding it to be back.

"Yes, it's great," he said when she returned the question. "Not that I didn't like Cow Village in its way, but... this is home. My people are here, I don't have to worry about hitting my head on the roof of the tunnel when I leave the house, no arguments about what kind of tomb to build. No offence, Bokka, but your village is a bit strange in those ways."

"I suppose it is," Bokka agreed. "We have our reasons. You're much more sheltered here – you'd build tunnels, too, if you got the kind of storms we get in the winter."

"I expect we would." With all that agreed, Sal went on his way. Bokka went on working on her stone ball, shaping it one fleck at a time, and Laki took a little flour out of the quern and started the next handful of wheat.

The next conversation was harder. A young man came over and introduced himself to Bokka, ignoring Laki even though she'd known him all his life. Perhaps *because* she'd known him all his life – his mother had been friends with her mother and she'd been there, along with his older siblings, when he was born.

"I'm Jeko," he said to Bokka.

"I'm Bokka."

"You're beautiful."

"Really?"

"The most lovely woman I've ever seen."

Bokka made a frowning face and looked down.

"You are beautiful, Bokka," Laki said quietly, taking a break from the quern. "But it doesn't mean you owe him anything."

"I didn't say—" Jeko began.

Laki held up a finger. "We heard what you said. And how you said it."

"You don't have any reason to stop me talking to our guest." Jeko gestured to Bokka, who was staring at the ground.

"I have every reason not to let you upset her." Laki hoped that sounded like general hospitality to Jeko, although she had much more personal reasons as well.

"She shouldn't be upset by a compliment." Turning back to Bokka, Jeko said, "You should look up and smile for me, with that lovely face. Come on, smile."

Bokka lifted her head and let her gaze go past his shoulder. She grinned a horrible grin which was more like the baring of teeth; the sides of her mouth moved outwards rather than upwards, and her eyes were empty.

"Never mind," Jeko muttered, and wandered away, deliberately casual to prove that he hadn't been scared.

"Never mind him," Laki said to Bokka when he was out of sight. She tried to distract Bokka by describing all the sheep they kept in Otter Village and where they grazed them, but Bokka didn't reply to anything.

Finally, as Laki was about to finish the wheat they'd brought out and call the job done for the day, Drom stopped by. "Sal said I'd probably still find you here."

"Here we are." Laki gave Drom a considering look. She had found Drom difficult sometimes when they were young – they'd both preferred working with the sheep or the cows to what they saw as boring jobs like grinding flour, and had once nearly come to blows over who got to take the cows out to graze in the woods – but as they grew up they'd also grown closer. Over the winter, when Smeka died, Drom's experience of loss in his own family had let him be a great support to Laki. Now she wondered whether he'd extend that support to Bokka. "Were you looking for us for anything particular?"

"Just that I hadn't seen you since you arrived," he said. He was casual, but Laki thought there was something artificial about it. "And I wanted to meet our new guest."

Bokka looked up for long enough to give him a nod.

"What do you think of Otter Village?" he asked. "Not that you've been here long enough to have a fully formed opinion, but first impressions."

"It's strange that you don't have more protection from storms," Bokka said. "When your people arrived in Cow Village, they all thought our covered spaces between houses very strange – but if it's raining, you have to go outside to visit a neighbour. It's much easier to be under cover when the wind is blowing sand across your houses, or the rain is pouring down, or the snow has settled."

Drom pulled an exaggerated face of thoughtful consideration. "I see what you mean," he said. "And what about the people? Does living that closely with your neighbours mean you're very close to them emotionally as well, or do they annoy you more?"

"I'm sure we're a closely bonded community," Bokka said. The phrase had a formal tone which made Laki think someone must have said it in a village meeting and Bokka had copied it.

"But the people there can be annoying," Laki commented, wondering if she could prompt Bokka into more honesty.

"So can people here," Bokka replied with a shrug.

Drom looked at Laki quizzically. "Jeko was here not long ago and he was... making some mistaken assumptions," she explained.

"Ah." Drom nodded. "He's got some more growing up to do."

*

That night, they held a big feast to welcome Bokka to the village and the traders home. Trebbi hadn't been going to—she said to Heln that nobody had been away that long and it would disrupt the routine of the village—but Laki overheard and spoke up. She wanted a welcome feast, and to make sure it didn't sound like she wanted it for herself, she explained that she wanted to show Bokka how much better such things went in Otter Village. Heln frowned at her, possibly because her description of Cow Village made it sound worse than it really was, but Trebbi shrugged and said they might as well. "We killed a cow a few days ago and there's meat left. Ask Dru to bring it over and you can start cooking."

Laki happily took charge of the meal. Bokka offered to stay in Trebbi and Aleuks' house and make the bread, and Laki happily accepted – one less thing to worry about – until she realised that it meant Bokka was hiding away in the house and not seeing the preparations for the feast at all. Laki got to see almost everyone in the village, and chat to them as they gathered and brought different bits of spare food or things which needed eating soon, but she couldn't talk to Bokka, or even show her what was happening.

And the bread seemed to be taking a long time. When the rest of the food was almost ready, and a few people were already eating limpets they'd roasted on the hearth stones, Laki went to find Bokka.

The bread was ready. A pile of fresh loaves sat in a basket next to Bokka, who was turning her half–made stone ball in her hand. It had come on a long way since the morning, Laki noticed. Bokka must have been working at it on and off all day. Now, she was looking at it carefully in the firelight, turning it this way and that. She didn't respond to Laki's entrance.

"Bokka," Laki said, thinking that she hadn't been heard. "Bokka, this bread looks great—and it smells great! The rest of the food is ready, too. There are some limpets, and a fish stew, and a salted beef stew, and some pieces of meat roasted on skewers."

"Okay," Bokka said. She didn't look up from the ball or move.

"Come outside and eat, then, and meet some more people from Otter Village." Laki tried to keep her voice positive and encouraging, not letting her confusion and irritation show.

Bokka shook her head. "I'm not hungry. Can I have some bread and stay in here?"

She could, Laki supposed, but it wasn't the point. "This is a welcome feast—mostly for you. They weren't going to do one because the rest of us came home. This is for you to see how much better Otter Village is!" Laki stopped there before her voice could rise any further.

"You really think this place is better than my home?" Bokka asked.

Laki had assumed they both did. "Yes. You agreed to come because it's better here, remember? Lots of people in Cow Village were being really mean to you. They bullied you, Bokka. People here are nice."

"But it's all different," Bokka said. She sounded on the verge of tears. "They're all strange, and whoever had a feast with four different foods! It's supposed to be one animal! And where are my parents? And everyone will talk and I won't understand and it will be loud and—" She cut herself off with a gasp, clutching the stone ball to her chest.

Not sure where to start, Laki took a step closer to see whether she could offer comfort. "It is different," she agreed. "But you're here because it's different—it's a good thing. And you won't get to see that unless you come out and meet people."

Bokka sighed. Laki wanted to hug her, to pull her up and take her outside or at least stroke her hair and help her feel better. She was wondering whether any of those were actually a good idea when Bokka stood up from her crouch. "I can bring my stone carving with me, right?"

"Of course."

"And you'll stay so I don't have to talk to someone new on my own?"

"If you like." Laki didn't think it would be necessary—she trusted the people of Otter Village—but it wouldn't be a hardship to stay near Bokka all evening.

"Okay." Bokka took a deep breath and pushed her shoulders back, adopting a posture which suggested confidence she clearly didn't feel. "And when I've eaten and talked to some people, can I go back to Trebbi's house and work on my stone ball before I go to sleep?"

"I expect so."

Bokka gave the sphere one last stroke with her fingers, then tucked it into the pouch at her belt where it normally lived. "Okay, then."

Laki reached out her hand. Bokka hesitated but Laki waved it, not moving from where she stood until Bokka took it. "We go together." They had got outside when Laki realised her mistake. "The bread!" She had to drop Bokka's hand as they went back for the baskets, but they were able to arrive at the feast together and were quickly welcomed by the hungry people who had gathered. Some had started eating but the extra bread was much needed.

At first, Bokka was focussed on eating and Laki had to do most of the talking. They chatted to Aleuks for a little while before she moved off to discuss some tree clearing in detail with Tauros.

Laki wanted to talk to Trebbi, but she was also busy with village business—something to do with someone from Dog Village who wanted to come and live in Otter Village.

While they were looking around, Jeko came back again. He ignored Laki again and sat down next to Bokka. "I'm the best stone worker in the village. I saw you're working on some little stone thing. Can I see?"

Bokka was visibly reluctant. "How's your mother these days?" Laki asked Jeko, hoping to change the subject. "I saw her in the distance yesterday but I haven't spoken to her since I got back."

"She's fine." Jeko shrugged. "I made her some really good flint tools while you were away and she's so proud of me, she's finishing hides ready for making into clothes much faster than before, and it's easier on her back. Now you've come back with this little girl and her fancy stone carving, and I want to see."

"Little?" Bokka spat. "What are you talking about, little boy?"

"What are you talking about, stranger? Show me what you brought!"

"No."

"I thought this was all about trading!" Jeko said. The raised voices had attracted a few glances and Laki saw him glance around, see the reaction, and moderate his posture and tone so others would think it was a friendly conversation. "I thought you came to trade, stranger," he said with a smile. "I'm not even asking to trade for it. All I want is to see what you've done."

The shift seemed to work on Bokka as well. She picked her stone ball from her pouch and held it out on the flat of her hand. Jeko picked it up. Bokka followed it with her hand—Laki thought she hadn't meant him to take it, only to look—but stopped short of snatching it back from him.

Turning it, Jeko saw the knobs and hollows, then the part where Bokka had only lightly sketched out the rest of the pattern. "It's not even finished," he said, turning his face away as if in disgust. Bokka took hold of it and he pulled slightly, before releasing it, so that she had to tug against his strength and wobbled a step backwards when he suddenly let go. "The best stone workers only show their work when it's finished. Let me know when you're ready, little one." He walked away.

Bokka recovered her balance and put the stone ball away. Laki wanted to say something—to apologise—but she didn't know how to explain.

"Who else have you known a long time?" Bokka asked, and Laki found herself introducing Dona, who had been her friend since childhood. They'd often gone out to watch the cows together, playing in the woods as the animals grazed around them, before Dona hurt her ankle falling out of a tree and couldn't walk so far. Now, Dona had a baby snuggled against her back and seemed smiling and happy.

She was also curious about Bokka, glancing at her several times while Laki asked about Dona's partner and her baby. Having got both their names and heard that the baby was strong and growing well, Laki gave in and introduced Bokka. "She's come from Cow Village to see how much nicer people are here."

Dona laughed, which was not the result Laki had been expecting. "Really? I'm sure people are the same everywhere, Laki."

"You don't know what they were like."

Dona turned to Bokka. "What do you think so far?" she asked. "Is Laki right? Are we completely different here, or just people who don't know you yet?"

"You don't understand," Laki interrupted, annoyed by her old friend's casual rejection of her perspective. "Some people in Cow Village were horrible to Bokka, really bullying her."

"People here can be bullies, too," Dona said calmly. "Besides, I think Bokka can speak for herself, can't she?"

Bokka shrugged. She could speak for herself, Laki knew, but perhaps she didn't want to. "Not bullies like—" Laki began.

"Who is a bully here?" Bokka asked, putting down her empty bowl. "You said people here can be bullies, too. Are they?"

"Well," Dona said, tearing off another piece of bread but not yet lifting it to her mouth. "Yes, I suppose they are. Sometimes. Not always, and not all of them."

"Not everyone in Cow Village is a bully," Bokka agreed. "My parents are nice to me. Aiso is nice to me."

"Only because you spend so much time helping him," Laki muttered. Dona gave her a little glare and handed her another piece of bread. It was a gesture they'd used for more years; *here, chew this, I'm talking.*

"Most people here are nice," Dona continued. "Most of them try and help. Lots of people helped Laki when her mother was ill, and lots of people help me with my baby, and most people were kind when I hurt my ankle – although some of them asked why I was climbing up the tree in the first place, since there wasn't any fruit to pick or anything, and that got a bit nasty after a while. They had a point, but they didn't need to keep saying it two moons later when I was limping around."

"They didn't really have a point," Laki said. She'd said it at the time as well, and Dona ignored her as usual.

"And Laki will have told you about the murder," Dona said, "and lately there's been some trouble about Tauros because he's been going back and forth between here and Dog Village during the night and people are worried that he's stirring up trouble against their leader."

"Well, people in Dog Village—" Laki started, but Bokka cut in.

"Murder?"

It was true, Laki supposed. There had been a murder, not long ago, and she hadn't mentioned it at all when she described Otter Village. It wasn't the way things normally were, and it hadn't seemed relevant.

"We've never had a murder in Cow Village," Bokka said. "Why would you bring me to a place with a murderer?"

"The murderer died as well," Dona hurried to assure her. Laki didn't know what to say and opted to take another large bite of bread instead of commenting.

"Still." Bokka turned to Laki. "Why didn't you tell me that? You lied to me! You were so sure everyone here was nice!"

"They are!" Laki felt her eyes fill with tears. She swallowed the last of her bread and added, "Everyone here now is nice, aren't they? Better than the way horrible Pru treated you in Cow Village!"

"Pru never killed anyone."

Even if that were true—and Laki had to accept that it probably, inconveniently, was—it wasn't the point. "Even if I missed something out, my lie isn't as big as yours was!"

"I didn't lie!" Bokka stood up suddenly. Laki noticed that they were attracting attention—not only from Dona, who was openly staring, but from other people eating nearby.

"You..." Laki started, then realised that she didn't want everyone in the village to know that she'd brought a thief to live with them. The others who had visited Cow Village already knew but it wasn't anyone else's business. "Never mind," she said instead, trying to keep her voice down. "I'm sorry I didn't tell you, but Peku's death seemed a long time ago to me, and as Dona said, the man who killed him is dead, too. There aren't any murderers here now and you don't have to worry."

Despite her best efforts, she had spoken loudly enough for several people nearby to hear her, and they now started to give their own comments. "It wasn't that long ago." "Definitely no murderers here now." "I could murder another stick of roast." "Bad things happen in every village." "That's right, nothing to worry about."

Bokka covered her ears, lowering her head. Laki glanced at Dona. Her desperation must have been visible because Dona, with the ease of long practice, shared out the jobs between them. She waved Laki towards Bokka with a single fluid gesture, at the same time as turning towards the other people who had spoken. "This makes me think of that old story about a man who visited a hundred villages," she began. "Does anyone remember...?"

Grateful to her friend for creating a distraction, Laki turned away. Bokka was already walking away from the fire and the village, along the path towards the bay. At first, Laki followed her. When they were far enough away from the others, though—when Laki could no longer hear chatter behind them and thought that any conversation they had wouldn't be heard—she began to wonder why Bokka wasn't stopping. Wasn't she going to turn round and talk? Was she really walking to the sea and not away from the people?

"Bokka!" Laki called, but Bokka didn't stop or even look round.

Laki had to decide whether to call again and hurry after her as the sun set and the night closed in, or stop following and leave Bokka to whatever she was planning to do alone.

"Bokka!" she called. The other woman was not so far away that she couldn't hear Laki if she wanted to listen. "Bokka, I'm going to go back to the village." Bokka's steps paused for a moment, but then she kept walking.

Okay, then. Laki let anger come in. She hadn't meant to lie. Bokka knew exactly what she was doing when she stole. To be upset with her was hugely unfair. She crossed her arms and stomped back to the fire, where Dona had saved her a share of the honeycomb which was passing round. They'd found a bee's nest in a tree the day before and managed to rescue some honey—not much, but enough for everyone to have a fingertip–sized piece. Laki let hers melt slowly in her mouth.

"Bokka didn't want to come back?" Dona asked.

"No," Laki said. She could have asked to save some honey for Bokka, but she didn't. "Did you get people to remember that story?"

"Some of it." Dona shrugged and leaned closer. "Are you okay? Is Bokka okay?"

"I hope so," Laki said, letting it stand for them both. "Probably a bit tired. Anyway, tell me about how you've been. What's it like having a baby?"

Chapter 11

IT HAD BEEN TOO MUCH. Bokka went to the sea, reassured that it was the same here as at home. She enjoyed the noise, which was regular, and unlike human noises, it didn't demand any reply. *It had been my own fault,* she thought. She hadn't wanted to go to the feast. Laki had encouraged her and she'd given in—that was the mistake. She should have stayed and eaten plain bread in Trebbi's house.

As her eyes adjusted to the dark, she was able to find a flat–topped rock above the tide line and sit comfortably. The waves washed in and out. She breathed in and out. Being around people was difficult sometimes. She took out the stone ball she was working on and turned it in her hand. The contrast of rough, unworked surfaces and smooth areas was soothing. There was a place where her thumb fitted naturally, as if the two had grown together. Bokka let herself focus on that satisfaction and let go of the anxiety about the conversation.

Laki would soon realise that she was being unreasonable. She would see that Bokka wasn't really better off here, and they would go back to Cow Village, and Laki would talk to Bokka in front of Pru and Pru would be upset and Bokka would have won. Bokka would wear Laki's necklace—openly, with permission, this time—and Pru would be so jealous of it she'd try and steal it, but Bokka would foil her cunning plan and everyone would laugh at Pru exactly the same way they had often laughed at Bokka. Pru would cry. Bokka pictured herself laughing in triumph.

It was a lovely dream. Bokka sighed and forced herself to let go of that picture, as well. Of course it would never happen like that. People sided with Pru because of who she was, not because of anything she'd done or not done. People disliked Bokka because of something innate about her which made her wrong all the time. Because she never knew what to say, and because she would rather work little pieces of stone than play games with the other children, and because she sometimes felt she had to steal things. So whatever Laki did or didn't do, they would like Pru and not Bokka. It was the way Goddess had arranged the world.

At least there was the sea. Bokka considered going for a swim, but although the night was warm with a gentle spring breeze, and the tide was slack, the darkness and the unknown rocks of a strange beach put her off. She wasn't ready to go back to the village either, though. Eventually she would have to go and find Laki. Would Laki really see her side of it? Probably not.

Her fingers found a rough patch on the ball, and she took a pebble out of her pouch, the one she liked to use for fine grinding work. It was slower in the dark—she had to touch the area regularly instead of looking to see how it was progressing—but she could work well enough.

She had the stone ball and the sea. She missed her parents and her familiar bed and the hopes she had harboured for Laki's support, but she reassured herself that she still had what she needed.

*

"Where's Bokka?" Trebbi asked as soon as she saw Laki moving.

Laki blinked at her, not fully awake.

"Bokka," Trebbi repeated. "Her bed is empty, doesn't look like it's been slept in. I can't see her nearby."

"Oh shit." The fur seemed to fight back, hanging heavy on Laki's shoulders and promising lovely warmth if she'd lie down again, but she managed to wrestle it off. "She didn't come back last night?"

"It doesn't look like it." Trebbi wasn't yelling but there was a thread of anxiety in her voice. "Did she stay in another house or something?"

"I don't know," Laki said.

"I thought you were with her."

"I was, mostly." Laki got to her feet. "She was with me most of the evening until Dona said... something that upset her. She wanted to be on her own for a while, so I let her go. I think she took the path towards the sea. And I came to bed. But I thought she'd come back."

"Yes," Trebbi said, giving Laki a look which conveyed all the questions she carefully wasn't asking about that story. "Anyway, you'd better go and look for her now, I think. Maybe she slept on the beach. But she might be cold; it was warm last night and then got chilly before the morning."

"I'll take a cloak for her." Laki picked up her own cloak but hung it over her arm rather than putting it on.

From the bed on the far side of the house Aleuks groaned questioningly, and Trebbi went to her. Laki left the house.

*

The stone ball was still in her hand, warmed by the constant contact, when she woke. Bokka wriggled a little, enough to lift her head and check that she was safe – well above the high tide line and on a flat piece of grassy ground, not up on a rock – before letting it drop back to the ground. She sighed deeply. She wished she was in Trebbi's house, or better yet, back in Cow Village in her parents' house. She wished she had something to eat.

Sitting up, she started to assess the bay for the makings of a meal. There was a little driftwood at the top of the beach, probably dry enough to burn, or she could walk up the path to the top of the cliff and into the woods. There were some limpets on the rocks. The tide was too high for rockpools, but perhaps she could find something else...

Bokka wondered whether she was really planning to live on the beach. At some point, wouldn't she have to go back to the village? She wanted to see Laki again, even though Laki hadn't told the truth, and she wanted to be warm and full of food again, but she didn't really want to deal with Jeko and Dona and the possibility of murder and all that.

Looking around, she spotted Heln's boat – or was it Aleuks' boat? She hadn't got that clear in her mind. They'd pulled it well up, secured it with ropes, and covered it against the weather, but it was by the shore, and it wouldn't be that much work to get it ready to sail again. She could paddle it back to Cow Village on her own.

Abandoning the limpet she had been trying to remove from a rock, Bokka went over to the boat. She lifted some of the branches off and revealed it. Larger than she remembered. Would she really be able to paddle it alone? She didn't have a choice. She needed to go home, and this was the way.

The boat was almost half uncovered when Bokka heard a noise. It wasn't a sea noise, or a bird noise. It came from towards the village. She froze, anxiously watching to see what was coming.

She glimpsed Laki's hair first, the thick curls unruly as if she hadn't combed it since she got out of bed.

Bokka considered her options. She could hide. She could try to cover the boat up again. Or she could carry on and ask Laki to join her. Or carry on and tell Laki to leave.

Her breath quickened as Laki turned a corner and came down the final slope towards the shore. That ruled out some of the options – too late to hide, too late to cover the boat up. She hadn't thought anyone would come looking for her.

"Bokka!" Laki called. "Bokka, are you okay? We didn't know where you were."

"You found me," Bokka pointed out. Laki must have seen her going down the path to the shore the night before and had a good idea where she was. "I'm fine."

"Really?" Laki asked, as she climbed over a rock to take the most direct route towards Bokka.

"Really," Bokka said. "A bit hungry, but I could cook some limpets if I wanted to."

Laki didn't reply but looked at her, and Bokka thought Laki was trying to convey something with her expression. Maybe Bokka was missing something. She shrugged, as much for herself as Laki, and turned away, back to the boat. She lifted off another of the thickly leaved oak branches which had been used to cover it.

"What are you doing?" Laki asked.

"I'm getting the boat ready to go home," Bokka said.

"Oh." Laki was quiet for a moment and Bokka continued her work. "Err... have you talked to Heln about this? Or Aleuks or anyone? Who's coming with you? When are you all leaving?"

"Nobody's coming with me," Bokka said. She had finished taking off the rain protection, and now set about untying the ropes which held the boat against strong winds. "I haven't talked to anyone. Except I'm talking to you now. I'm leaving as soon as I can."

"You..." Laki said, and, "But..." She seemed to be struggling with what to say. Bokka could understand that.

"You don't need to say anything," Bokka reassured her. "I made a mistake when I agreed to come, and I'm putting it right, that's all. Nothing to worry about."

Laki didn't seem to agree. Tears were running down her face. "No, Bokka," she said. "Can you stop, for a moment, please? Stop and let's talk about this."

"Talk about what?" Bokka asked, but she did stop untying the ropes. There were two left, and the knots were damp with dew and difficult.

"About... you leaving," Laki said. "Firstly, it's not your boat, you can't take it. Secondly, even if you did, you can't sail it with one person—Heln and Aleuks say they struggle with the two of them, and they know it better than anyone else. Thirdly, where are you going to go? And..." Laki's posture changed and her voice shifted, too, becoming deeper and the words slower. "What's this all about? Why do you want to go?"

128

"I'm going to go home," Bokka said, determined to take the questions in order. "This is all about me leaving here and going back to Cow Village. I want to go because you told me it would be nice here and it's not." She looked at Laki's necklace and imagined how it would be warmed by the skin underneath it. Laki was still wearing the tunic she slept in, and she'd picked up a cloak but not put it on; it was hanging over her arm. Bokka wondered why. Had she run so fast down the path that it was too hot?

"But it is." Bokka turned away when Laki said that; there was no point trying to explain it. Laki had a good point about the boat being too big for one person. Perhaps there was another way to get to Cow Village. Could she walk? No, there had been at least one channel between islands. Maybe she could walk to another village and find a boat there. Maybe she could build a boat. Skins would be hard to get but a small boat made from a single log, she could do that. It would take a long time but the principle of hollowing out the log was the same as the hollows between knobs on her stone ball.

Laki was still speaking. "Bokka," she said, "Bokka, are you listening to me?"

"No."

Bokka knew people thought it was rude to say that, but it was true, and in any case, she was separating from Laki and no longer putting any weight on what she said. She watched Laki, waiting for her to throw up her hands in disgust and yell and stride away.

Laki didn't do that. She stared at Bokka for a while—longer than Bokka thought was normal—and shrugged her shoulders. "Okay. Why not?"

"It wasn't true," Bokka explained, "what you said, about people being nicer here." Laki just looked at her, so Bokka went on. "Not the thing about the murderer – he's dead. You could have mentioned it, but it's in the past. But Jeko, yesterday."

"He was rude," Laki admitted.

"And Dona."

"Dona's nice?"

"Dona's not nice." This was hard. Bokka took the half—made stone ball from her pouch and rolled it between her hands. "Or maybe she's trying to be nice. She's probably nice to you. But to me she's the same as all the other people. She can be friendly or rude or ignore me and I still won't understand her. She won't know why I'm doing what I'm doing."

"Do the people in Cow Village know why you do the things you do?"

"Of course not!" Bokka shook her head, hard.

"Does anyone?"

Not really. Bokka didn't say that aloud, instead running through the implications of it: if nobody understood her, and so nobody could be nice to her, she had nowhere to go and would need to live the rest of her life alone. She would have all the time she needed to make that wooden boat. She would have to hunt and cook for herself and grow her own wheat and weed her own fields and never have time to work on a boat, let alone a stone ball, at all.

When she opened her eyes, Laki was closer than before.

"I'm trying to understand," Laki said softly.

Bokka tried to work out whether that was true. Hearing about the murder had put everything Laki said in a new perspective: could she be trusted? Bokka thought that Laki probably genuinely thought she was trying to understand, but that it wasn't possible. Nobody had ever really understood her.

She'd been quiet for too long, thinking, and Laki had started talking again. "I want to understand," she said. "I need you to explain to me, to help me, but I am trying. It takes time, but I'm sure I can understand."

"I don't think so." Laki had been coming closer, so Bokka turned and walked away, down the beach to the edge of the waves. "You don't even know why I'm trying to leave again."

"Because—" Laki started.

"And you don't need to know. I don't need you to know. I need you to help me get home." She looked out across the water, to where the waves crashed on half–hidden rocks as the tide moved past them, and tried to work out the route a boat would take.

"I still want to know." Laki didn't move, which Bokka felt was an improvement. "But okay, I don't need to know right now. You need to go home. I'm sorry, Bokka. I was trying to help."

Bokka nodded. That was likely to be true.

"Give me a few days," Laki went on. "I'll need to talk to some people, find out if anyone's planning another trading trip. We might have to go to another village first."

"I'll be here," Bokka said. She gestured along the cliffs. "There are some nests up there. If I get any eggs, I'll bring them up to the village to be cooked."

*

Halfway up the path, Laki stopped and turned back. She could see Bokka, barefoot and without her cloak or tunic which might catch on the stone, climbing nimbly up the cliff. Probably Bokka would come down with a pouch full of eggs, but would she be willing to change her mind about going home? Was it even worth trying to persuade her?

Laki shook her head and sighed, then turned her back on Bokka and walked up to the houses. The village was busy with early morning tasks: heating water for cooking and washing, one or two people getting their flour started for the day, some sitting and chatting as they ate. Laki asked after Trebbi and was directed to the sheep pens.

She opened her mouth to start to explain but found herself in a flood of tears instead.

"Laki, what is it? What happened? Did you find her? Is she hurt? Is she..."

Laki managed to shake her head before Trebbi could assume the worst. "On the beach. She's fine, at least her body is. She..." She wants to go home, Laki tried to say. She wants to leave me. She doesn't see the good here. She has grabbed onto this thing about what happened to Peku and she's making it into a huge problem, when it's only one part of the village story, and of course I didn't mention it because why would I?

Trebbi put an arm around her shoulders. "If she's alive, we can work on everything else," she said. "Come on, Laki. I've looked at these sheep. Ghoilos, they're all fine, that cut on the lamb's leg is healing nicely, you can take them out. Go up towards the tomb, to that grassy spot under the elm. Tauros will come and check how you're doing in the middle of the day. I'm going out to the western fields to see if we need to weed them again, or if they'll get to harvest. Come on, Laki, walk with me."

Thus gently encouraged among Trebbi's busy day, and mostly ignored as people greeted Trebbi as they walked through the village, Laki simply walked and focussed on breathing, and by the time they had left the houses behind them, she was calm enough to talk.

"Bokka wants to leave," Laki explained to Trebbi and described the main points of their conversation. "I'd told her that people were nicer here, but she says they're not."

Trebbi shrugged. "Some communities are better or worse—the stories we're hearing from Dog Village at the moment are pretty bad—but Aleuks says, when you travel, you still have to take yourself with you."

"You think Bokka's problem is herself?"

"Perhaps." Trebbi paused as they reached the first of the wheat fields, shading her eyes to look out over it. "Or perhaps how others have made her feel about herself. But that's not really for us to solve. I'm not sure we can take her home again for a while. Nobody was planning to go trading, and although we might go to the great stones for a celebration and a market in the autumn, that's several moons away and we wouldn't be going as far north as Cow Village."

"What else can we do?"

"Let her be?" Trebbi suggested. She bent to pull out a weed from the edge of the field. There were plenty to find if someone wanted to come and weed, Laki thought, but the question was whether there were so many that work became a top priority. "It's a big change – from home, to travelling with four other people, to getting to know a new village."

"Aleuks and Heln seem to manage well enough," Laki said, "and I was fine visiting Cow Village."

"Aleuks and Heln chose the travelling life." Trebbi turned to her, sympathetic. "And different people take these things different ways. Give Bokka some time for Goddess to act in her life."

"What if she really steals the boat? What if I shouldn't have left her alone by the shore?"

"You couldn't have brought her up here, so you had to leave her." Trebbi was always refreshingly practical. "Anyway, these fields will be fine for a while, probably another ten days or so. We'll put our effort into getting the next lot of beans sown." She led Laki back towards the village.

When they got there, Laki planted beans. The soil had been prepared and they sowed the beans in pairs, each pair in a little hole with a stick to mark it. She thought about going down to the shore. Each time she straightened up and looked towards the sea, though, she imagined Bokka feeling more anxious than happy to see her and went back to her work.

Chapter 12

BOKKA HAD FOUND SOME EGGS. She climbed down from the cliff and looked at them, nestled on some moss in one of her pouches, but she wasn't hungry, and she couldn't bring herself to walk up the path to the village.

Instead, she sat and watched the sea again. She had to make a decision, she realised: to trust Laki again, and wait for someone to agree to travel to Cow Village with her, or to strike out on her own. She hadn't covered the boat back up. She could set off in it right now. Well, in a while when the tide was high again.

If she did nothing, she was effectively waiting for Laki.

The waves came and went.

Bokka watched them, and after a while she felt calm again. She took out her stone ball. She found a pebble on the beach which would make a good new hammer stone and pecked away at the curve of another knob. It felt good to shape something under her hands. Focussed on the stone ball, with the sea in the background, she could ignore where she was. She was making, and breathing, and everything felt right again.

She'd been sitting there for some time—the sun was high in the sky—when a noise startled her. She looked round and saw Jeko coming down the path. "I thought I'd find you here, little girl."

Bokka didn't have anything to say about that. She didn't know why he would have thought about her at all. Rather than replying, she went back to her work on the stone ball.

"I won't go away just because you ignore me, you know." Jeko stood immediately in front of her, feet planted by her feet, close enough to touch. Bokka definitely didn't want to do that, but she couldn't move away without getting even closer to him. She leaned backwards instead, aware that if she leaned much further, she would fall backwards.

"What will make you go away?" she asked.

Jeko laughed and Bokka knew she'd made a mistake. "Look at me," he said.

Bokka felt that she couldn't see much of anything else, but she lifted her head a bit from the stone ball to his chest.

"What have you got there? Some kind of ball?" Jeko reached down and snatched it from her hands. "Oh, neat, it's carved. Oh, wait, it's not finished. Useless." He chucked it over his shoulder, and Bokka heard the knock as it landed against another stone.

The idea that it might be broken overwhelmed everything else. She stood up, straight into Jeko, and shoved him out of the way. He stumbled backwards and fell onto a patch of seaweed, yelping. Bokka ignored him and went to pick up her stone ball.

The carved knobs were intact. It had chipped slightly with the impact, but on the side she hadn't yet finished; the material which was lost was stone she would eventually have carved away anyway. It was okay. She cradled it in her hands, running her fingers over every surface again and trying to calm down.

Jeko got up again. He brushed bits of dry seaweed off his richly decorated tunic and looked Bokka up and down. "Not only rude and useless, but also violent."

Why did he need to say that out loud? Bokka had been taught to keep her real opinions to herself. She opened her mouth to say that he was the one who was rude and nasty but decided that might fall under the same rule. Instead, she turned and started to walk away.

"You can't go back to the village," Jeko said behind her. "I'll tell them all what you did."

She had started up the path away from the beach, but that gave her pause. What would happen if he told them? At first, she didn't see why it would matter. She'd simply given him a push, and he'd fallen. He wasn't hurt or anything.

"They'll see that you're a violent cow." He was close behind her. She walked forward a bit further but couldn't escape his voice. "They'll tell Laki she was wrong to bring you, and she'll never talk to you again, and you'll have to go off on your own to walk all the way back to your horrible Cow Village where I hear they're all pushers and shovers like you."

Bokka tried to sort through everything he was saying. Never seeing Laki again would be bad. But she'd lived without Laki before. Going off on her own, walking home, was the plan anyway, if she couldn't use a boat. Only some of the people in Cow Village were horrible. But some of them were really horrible. But so was Jeko, and he was right here.

He was right there, in fact, so close behind her that she could hear his breathing. He put a hand on her shoulder. She'd stopped walking – big mistake. She shook herself hard, so he removed his hand, and then ran, as fast as she could, up the path and round the corners and into the village.

She almost ran bodily into Trebbi, who emerged from one of the houses without warning. She only narrowly managed to swerve in time to brush Trebbi's shoulder and come to a stop.

"Bokka!"

Surprise, or anger? Bokka wasn't sure. She hung her head, panting, looking at the stone ball still in her hand.

"Bokka, what's the matter? Why were you running?"

"I... Jeko..." She looked around, expecting Jeko to be immediately behind her and starting his version of the story as soon as he could.

He was nowhere to be seen. "What about Jeko?" Trebbi asked. "Is he okay? Was he hurt?"

"No, no, he wasn't hurt at all, he fell onto seaweed, it's bouncy." Bokka went to put the stone ball back in a pouch at her belt and found something else. "Here. I came to give you these." She lifted out the eggs carefully. One had cracked but there were still four green eggs with brown speckles, warm and round and good to eat.

Trebbi took them. "Okay, let's put these in a bowl." She called into her house for Aleuks, who came out carrying a wooden bowl lined with dry moss.

*

Planting beans was useful and not difficult. At first Laki gave it her full attention, making sure the stick went in at the perfect angle to support the beans later when they grew tall, but as she got into a rhythm, her mind wandered. She pictured Bokka alone on the beach and wondered whether she should go and find her. Had Bokka got some eggs from the cliff? Had she found somewhere to cook them? Was she alone? Was she enjoying being alone or wishing that Laki had stayed?

Was she right that Laki had made a horrible mistake in bringing her to Otter Village? Laki imagined trying to explain again. *I only wanted to help you. I only wanted to give you a choice. I only wanted to let you get away from the way Pru treated you.* The Bokka she was picturing didn't relent, only shook her head sadly and went back to untying the ropes on the boat. It was too late. The mistake had been made.

The desolation settled in Laki's chest. Tears ran down her cheeks and she sniffed, wiping her face with the back of her hand, trying to stop them falling to the ground. Some tears probably wouldn't do the beans any harm, but they probably wouldn't help, either. It occurred to Laki that she was terrible at looking after things—she'd wanted to help Bokka and couldn't—and the beans probably wouldn't grow, either.

"What's the matter?"

It was Heln's warm voice. Laki hadn't heard em come up behind her, but she recognised eir voice at once.

"I'm..." She didn't want to tell Heln that it might have been wrong to bring Bokka here. She'd been so glad when she was able to convince em to bring Bokka with them in the first place. "I'm fine."

"It's the beans which are making you cry?" Heln asked. Ey was smiling at her, teasing.

"Yes, I'm upset by the tragedy of having to bury these lovely beans in lots of holes in the ground." She gave Heln her best approximation of a grin and bent down to put the next two beans in their appropriate hole.

Heln pushed a stick in next to the beans she'd planted. "Absolutely terrible, isn't it?"

"The sadness of the beans going into the soil, the bare elegance of the sticks next to them, the as yet unfilled promise of bean flowers and more beans to come..."

"All a beautiful counterpoint to something else which made you cry." They did the next pair of beans as before.

"Yeah, I'm not actually that upset about beans," Laki admitted.

"So, what is it?" Rather than answer, Laki bent down to make the hole for the next pair of beans. "Okay, if you won't tell, I'll guess. Being back at home isn't the way you hoped it would be. Bringing Bokka here hasn't worked out the way you hoped it would. You're wondering if you should have made different choices."

Her head snapped up. "Who told you?"

"Nobody." Heln shrugged. "I mean, Sal told me that went he went past the bay this morning, the boat had been partially uncovered and untied, and Aleuks told me Bokka didn't sleep at the house last night. But neither of them had made anything of it. Seeing you having a cry over something was an extra clue."

Laki bent down again. In her surprise, she'd dropped the handful of beans she was holding and now needed to pick them all off the ground. "Well, you're basically right."

"So add the pattern to the pot for me."

"People here are nicer, in many ways, but I suppose when I imagined being here... I imagined people knowing Bokka the way they know me, the way I'm getting to know Bokka, and of course they don't, yet, and Bokka doesn't seem to want to give them time to learn. And she was upset, I suppose maybe frightened, when she heard about what happened to Peku."

"But that's all over," Heln said.

. "That's what I thought." Laki had her beans back and moved on to sowing the next pair. "I hadn't mentioned it, because... well, I hadn't thought of it. It hadn't come up, it didn't seem relevant, I didn't think, *someone needs to know this before they arrive in Otter Village.* But when Bokka found out, she thought I should have told her. I think it made her look at everyone in Otter Village in a different way."

"And she thought she'd be safer from a murderer down by the shore than sharing a house with three people?"

"I don't know," Laki said. They'd reached the edge of the field, and she straightened up and looked around. "Do you think there's space for another row before the trees?"

Heln walked along the side of the field a few paces. It had been cleared to a roughly straight line, but here and there hazels had been left and they spread over where the beans would be planted. "Probably not," ey said. "They'll get trampled when people come for the hazelnuts."

"Won't the beans be over by then?"

Heln shrugged. "I'm not sure."

"Well, my back says we can break there, and if Trebbi wants us to add some more, we can do that later." Laki stretched up to the sky. "Oh, Heln, what can I do about Bokka?"

"Have you asked Trebbi?"

"She told me to be patient," Laki said, and Heln rolled eir eyes with a little chuckle. "I know, typical Trebbi. And she says there may or may not be people travelling to the autumn gathering of the island villages, and maybe Bokka can go with them and hope to meet a party from Cow Village there..."

"A long wait and a lot of chances," Heln observed. "And what do you want to do?"

"I want to put it right." Laki picked up a bundle of spare bean support sticks and tapped the ends on the ground to emphasise her point. "If I made a mistake, I want to put it right. Bokka wants to go back to Cow Village, so I want to take her."

There was a pause, and Laki found Heln's eyes on her face, considering. She met eir gaze squarely.

"Quite right," ey said. "And I don't see any reason not to. I'll come with you, and probably Marko, too."

It was the exact opposite of what Laki had been expecting, and it was like the sunshine bursting through after a heavy shower of rain. "You will?"

"Why not? I'd been planning to be away, trading, for much longer than we were. And," Heln added with a grin, "better to go with the boat than have Bokka steal it from us."

Laki tried to laugh, not sure whether ey knew how close to the truth ey were. "Better," she agreed.

*

Everything seemed to move quickly after that. Laki felt like she'd been picked up by a stream, flowing quickly after a heavy rain. She and Heln got back to the village to find Bokka shaping dough into flat circles for cooking while Trebbi cut slices of meat. Heln waited until Aleuks and Marko joined them for the evening meal, then explained that ey'd been talking to Laki and would be happy to go trading again.

"I can take them to Cow Village and go on. That was the original plan, before we found the rams, and there's plenty of summer season left. We'll meet you at the autumn fair and travel home together."

Marko was nodding along. Laki wondered whether he'd had some idea that Heln would say this; they hadn't had a chance to speak since her discussion with Heln in the bean field, but Marko seemed to have no questions or hesitations.

Aleuks, on the other hand, had a lot to say. She wanted to know who would crew the boat. She wanted to know where they were going and when and why. She wanted to know everything. Heln answered the early questions patiently, saying that ey would ask Sal again, or perhaps they would manage with fewer people, or they would swap crews between villages. "Lots of people want to travel," ey said.

"And what about Laki? Does she want to travel, or is she staying in Cow Village?"

Heln hadn't been concerned about that, and ey turned to Laki for the answer. Laki, unfortunately, didn't know. She glanced at Bokka, hoping for a clue, but Bokka was wiping meat juices out of her bowl with some bread and didn't look up.

"You'd have to ask permission from the leader and people there, even if you wanted to stay," Trebbi said.

"Do I need to decide now?" Laki asked, and Aleuks allowed that it didn't matter, that she could stay there or come back to Otter Village as she pleased.

"Do we need to have a village meeting?" Laki asked Trebbi when the conversation paused.

"I don't think so," Trebbi said. Laki didn't know whether to be pleased or sad. It made things simpler and probably quicker, but she had wanted Bokka to see what they were like here. An Otter Village meeting was very different, and in Laki's opinion much better, than a Cow Village meeting. "We haven't had one to formally welcome Bokka, so we don't need one now that we're saying goodbye—unless you especially want it, Bokka."

Bokka shook her head firmly. "Not too many people."

And that was it settled. The conversation moved on to something Marko had seen in the woods, some sort of unusual bird. Laki stopped listening, watching Bokka instead. She had been quieter than usual, and when she'd finished eating, she didn't take out her stone ball as she usually would whenever her hands were empty. Instead, she cleared up the bowls and cooking pots and started washing them. "I'll do that later," Aleuks said, but Bokka wasn't to be stopped and nobody tried very hard.

Trebbi was called away to see some wheat which might have gone bad. Heln and Marko said their farewells and went to check on the boat before bed. Aleuks discovered that she needed to fetch fresh water and went to do that before it got dark. Laki and Bokka were left alone by the embers of the cooking fire.

"Do you want to build it up again?" Laki asked Bokka.

"No, people will come and think we want to sit around and talk," Bokka said, which was probably true. People in Otter Village—maybe people everywhere—loved to come for a fireside chat as the summer sun went down.

On the other hand, Laki did want to talk. She especially wanted to talk to Bokka.

"Can we huddle up, then?" Laki suggested. The temperature dropped as the sun went down, even on summer evenings, and she had already wrapped her cloak around her shoulders.

Bokka looked across the fire at her measuringly and replied slowly. "I suppose we could."

"If you'd like." Laki held one side of her cloak open. "Where's your cloak, anyway? You'll be cold without it."

"I left it by the bay."

"Marko and Heln will probably find it and bring it up soon," Laki said.

Bokka shook her head. "Jeko probably took it."

"Jeko? Why?"

Sighing, Bokka leaned against Laki's side, and Laki settled an arm around her shoulders. "He came to find me," Bokka explained, and started to tell the whole story. It came out in bits and pieces, and Laki let it come, trying to lay it out in her mind like pieces of leather she was going to sew into leggings. As she started to imagine what had happened, she also saw how much worse it could have been.

"What do you think he wanted?" she asked Bokka, but Bokka had no idea.

"I assume he was trying to cause trouble."

"I suppose so," Laki said, and decided to keep to herself the suspicion that he had wanted something more specific from Bokka.

"Anyway, he won't bother me anymore when we go back to Cow Village."

"Yeeessss..." The way Laki drew out the word made Bokka turn towards her.

"We are going back to Cow Village, aren't we?"

"Yes." Laki took a deep breath and pushed on as if through thick undergrowth, "But I was wondering what we should do after that."

"After Cow Village? I thought we were going to stay there."

"I suppose we could." Laki leaned over until she could rest her head on Bokka's shoulder. Bokka stroked her hair. "But I'm worried I won't be welcome to stay. I know you want to see Klamro and Nerto again, and we'll do that, and I know things aren't as easy here as I'd hoped they would be. But are Genu and Pru really going to welcome me to live in Cow Village?"

"What would you do?"

"I don't know."

Bokka's hand went still. Laki thought she should sit up, but she couldn't find the strength. "Do you... want to stay... in the same place as me?"

The slow and careful phrasing made Bokka's anxiety obvious. "Yes," Laki said. Her arm was loosely around Bokka's back, where it had slipped down from Bokka's shoulders, and now Laki tightened her embrace until she was pulling Bokka close against her. "Bokka, I want to be with and I want people to be nice to you. That's why I asked you to come here."

"But you'd forgotten the murder," Bokka pointed out, "and you'd not included Jeko in your plans." She wasn't returning Laki's hug.

"True." *I should move away*, Laki thought again, but she was warm and comfortable. "I'm sorry, I should have thought it through better. I wanted to help."

"I think you did help." Bokka's arm moved behind Laki. "Err, do you want me to...?"

"I'd like it if you hugged me."

"Good." Bokka wrapped both arms around Laki and squeezed her. Laki returned it, gently, and Bokka said, "Harder. I like it when you hold me tight."

They were almost sitting in each other's laps. The sky was red with sunset and Laki realised that soon they would lose the light. Would it matter? It would be hard to tidy up the bowls and things, but maybe they could be left for the morning. Laki decided not to worry about that unless Bokka brought it up. Instead, she nuzzled Bokka's neck as if trying to wriggle her way even closer.

"This feels good," Bokka said softly.

"Yeah."

"You did help. I would never have left Cow Village. I've seen so many new places. I've got an idea for a ball carved with lots of little knobs like the bumpy waves between the islands... I enjoyed the journey. But it's hard for me to fit in here."

"Yes," Laki said again, and sighed. Bokka squeezed her again—that did feel good. Laki could see why Bokka liked it.

"So do you want us to end up in the same place?"

"I wish we could go off alone, nobody but the two of us." Laki waved a hand southward towards the sea, suggesting long journeys. "You and me and a little boat, and we'd go from village to village, and we wouldn't have to choose where to live."

"Or we could find a place where nobody lives," Bokka said. "We could find an empty bay with a little beach and a clearing beside the woods, and we could build a house and grow some wheat and be the two of us forever."

"We'd have two cows and take them to market to be covered by the bull." The image was building in Laki's mind. "We'd grow a little plot of beans and find crabs on the shore and pick hazelnuts in the woods."

"We'd never have to talk to anyone else." There, that was what Bokka really wanted. And after what had happened, who could blame her? "We can't really, though, can we?"

"Well," Laki said, "maybe we could work towards it. You're right, I don't think we can avoid all people forever. We'd still need to meet people from a village sometimes – we couldn't manage a whole herd with just two of us, and we wouldn't need to, but you can't really keep two cows on their own. We might be able to spend more time just the two of us, though. If we became traders who travel around, or... I don't know, if we practiced hunting and went off into the woods for days at a time."

"I could make axe-heads and you could take them to market."

"We could catch crabs and trade them for other food."

"Do you think we could really escape from other people?"

Laki shook her head, although it only had the effect of rubbing her cheek against Bokka's shoulder. "Probably not, or not entirely. And you don't want to entirely, anyway—you want to see your parents again, at least."

"I do. And I want to spend time with one other person." Bokka lifted her hand to Laki's face and stroked gently down, along Laki's neck and around the line of her necklace. It made Laki shiver in a way that Bokka misinterpreted. "I'm sorry, you're cold. We should go inside."

"We could," Laki said, "but that's not why I shivered." She reached for Bokka's cheek and gently turned her face; she kissed the corner of Bokka's lips briefly and lightly, not wanting to go too far if Bokka wasn't interested.

Bokka turned towards her. In moments they were kissing deeply, tongues exploring mouths and hands reaching into tunics. They kissed urgently until they were breathless.

"Perhaps we should go in now," Laki panted.

They went. Aleuks might be back soon, so Laki guided Bokka straight to the bed. Bokka followed her lead, stripping off her clothes and letting them fall to the floor. Lifting up one of the furs on her bed, Laki said, "After you."

It was a bit small for them both. Bokka had tried to lie on her side, but her knees stopped Laki getting in as well. "On your back?" Laki suggested. That worked better because Laki could kneel astride her, Bokka's feet resting on the upright stone at the foot of the bed and Laki's knees planted each side of Bokka's hips on the heather–filled mattress. Lots of access, Laki noted, her hand exploring as she bent her head to kiss Bokka again.

Bokka was more hesitant, beginning to touch Laki at her neck where the bone and tooth beads still rested on her warm skin. From there, Bokka moved up first to stroke the smooth curves of Laki's cheek. "I should put that shape in a carving," Bokka murmured. "It feels so good."

"This one, too," Laki said, holding Bokka's breast and flicking her thumb lightly back and forth over Bokka's nipple. It made Bokka's body twitch with sensation, and those twitches pushed her pubic bone against Laki's vulva, and Laki curled her hips forwards and moaned with pleasure.

"Where should I touch you?" Bokka's hand had started to move down, but much too slowly. Laki took it and guided it rapidly over her breasts and hips, and into the heat of her wet core. Bokka rubbed experimentally. Laki pushed Bokka's hand harder against her clitoris, grinding down on it. "Do me, too," Bokka said before Laki kissed her again.

Their wrists bumped and they wriggled a bit to accommodate both hands between their legs. "There, there" Laki gasped as Bokka found the sweet spot. Being stroked with those strong fingers which made and polished so many beautiful things was exquisite. Laki's body was soon reaching a peak. She moaned into Bokka's neck and almost wept as the wave of pleasure swept over her.

She didn't mean to stop touching Bokka, but her hand went limp as she came. "Please keep going," Bokka whispered and, "Kiss me some more" when Laki managed to get her muscles moving again.

It was glorious to have Bokka thrusting against her hand and hips. Laki felt a distant sadness over the plan which had not worked out but hopeful for the future. And in that moment, everything was as she wanted it to be: her body sated, her lover panting, in a house which felt entirely safe.

"So close," Bokka said. "So good." Laki worked her wrist a little, seeking the right spot and pressing harder when Bokka gasped more loudly. "Yes. Yes. Enough."

She pulled at Laki's hand and shoulder—no more sex, Laki interrupted, but hug and kiss. That felt amazing, too. They kissed and hugged for a long time until Laki's knees ached. Regretfully, she nudged Bokka to rearrange their bodies, until Laki was curled into a tight ball in the middle of the bed with the slightly taller Bokka wrapped around her like a cloak.

They were almost asleep when Laki heard Aleuks open the door. She checked that the furs covered them, decided the clothes didn't matter, and slept without dreaming.

Chapter 13

LAKI FOUND THAT SHE WAS LOOKING at Cow Village differently as she arrived the second time. It was no longer a strange new place and an exciting adventure; it was full of memories—the place where she had left her clothes and her necklace disappeared, the path up to the headland where she had first talked to Bokka alone, the houses of people she liked or didn't like rather than merely didn't know.

Bokka ran to the village, calling for her parents. Heln, Marko, and Laki followed more slowly, carrying their gifts and other bags.

Pru was the first to appear. "You again?" she said to Bokka, which was the sort of reception Laki had feared.

Bokka either missed or decided to ignore the tone of it. "Yes, back to visit," she said breezily, walking right past Pru and continuing to call for Nerto and Klamro.

"You won't find them until they come back this evening. They're out with the sheep somewhere," Pru said.

She said it loudly enough for Bokka to hear. Bokka immediately took off running for the fields.

"And the rest of you?" Pru asked, stepping forward to block the path. "What are you doing here?"

"We came to visit, too," Heln said. Ey stepped forward with eir hands full of best quality furs. "Could you let your father know that we're here?"

"Difficult," Pru said. Her face was blank, but Laki had a premonition that bad news was coming. "He died."

"I'm so sorry."

"At least he'll be the first to be buried in the tomb he planned, as soon as we've finished it." Pru's voice was tense, and she didn't quite succeed in making this sound like an advantage. "And I'm the village leader now. What makes you think I'm going to let you visit?"

"We hoped we would be welcome, as we bring gifts and things to trade, on our way past to other villages." Heln and Marko had agreed on this story in advance; they could go on to another few villages and come back when the moon was the same shape again to give Laki and Bokka some time to work out whether they could live in Cow Village.

"Well, you're not."

Heln gave her a long look, but Pru wasn't moving.

"We can camp on the beach and move on tomorrow," Laki said, already annoyed with Pru's attitude.

"We could help you build the tomb," Marko said suddenly. He had been behind the others, but now Heln moved aside and let Marko come forward. "You said you need to finish the tomb before Genu can be buried in it. Wouldn't some extra hands be really useful? I've built with stone before—built houses and mended walls. We've all done heavy work. If you let us stay for a few days, and we spend our time helping with the tomb, your father will be buried the way he wanted sooner than you expected, and your village will be able to go back to its normal work."

"We don't need your help." It was what Pru would have said to any offer, Laki suspected.

Marko opened his mouth to expand on the offer—which was a good way in many ways—but Heln held up a hand. "Thank you," ey said. "We'll go back to the beach and camp by our boat tonight. We'll be gone in the morning."

Ey turned and walked away. Marko followed.

"Make sure you are." Pru scowled at them, then turned her back and left.

Laki paused, trying to look along the path past Pru to where Bokka had gone, wanting to ask someone to tell Bokka where they were, but Heln called her. "Laki, come with us." She had to go.

"Bokka won't know—" Laki whispered, not patient enough to wait until they were out of Pru's hearing.

"Bokka knows the village and the area," Heln said calmly. "She'll think of the boat and look for us."

"What if she doesn't come before—" Laki stopped when Heln raised eir hand again. They walked all the way back to the beach, out of sight of the village, before Heln spoke again.

"We know the area well enough, too," ey said. "We'll wait here for a while, because Pru might think to check on us. Someone in the village—probably Pru herself—will make sure Bokka knows where we are, if only to hurt her. And if Bokka doesn't come here before dark, you can go into the village this evening. Be cautious, be quiet, but you know where Bokka's parents live. She'll be there for the night, and you can probably slip in to talk to her."

They made themselves comfortable at the top of the beach. Marko went wandering to find some supplies—fresh water from a stream coming down to the shore, a crab, handfuls of fresh kelp which had been washed ashore and could be cooked and eaten. Laki didn't feel up to that. It made her think of Bokka, and that made her wish it was dark already, although she wasn't as confident as Heln about the plan to sneak in and see Bokka at night.

When she asked, "What if I get caught?" for the third time, Heln shrugged and sighed. Ey'd given eir best answers already. Instead, ey said, "Watch the boat," and went to help Marko collect driftwood for a cooking fire.

They made their food last a long time, breaking open every last part of the crab and scraping every last morsel of porridge from the bowls with their fingers. By the time the sun was setting, they were well fed and comfortable. The sky was clear and Heln had decided they didn't need to put up any tents; they would sleep in their furs, and it would be easy to get moving in the morning.

Laki was trying to get ready to go. They were far enough from the village that she couldn't hear whether things had gone quiet yet; she tried to picture the path because she didn't want to trip and fall alone in the dark.

She was wishing that they had a better idea when she heard voices coming towards them. Her first thought was that Pru had decided to come and cause more trouble, but as she sprang to her feet, she realised it was the opposite: Bokka ran towards her, and they hugged.

"It's shameful to leave guests outside the village like this," Nerto said. Ey and Klamro had been following along, and when Bokka released Laki, she greeted them, too.

"Well, we can welcome you to our fire," Heln said. It was unusual—Laki thought unheard of—but ey made it sound like a standard practice, giving eir words a formal intonation. "Please, join us, and we can offer you food."

"No food needed," Klamro said.

"A bowl of beer?" They didn't have much in the boat, so Laki thought that was a generous offer on Heln's part.

"If you wish, but we mostly came to talk."

Marko went to the boat to fetch a leather bag full of barley brew while Heln took a seat again on a rock. Laki gave Bokka's hand a tug and they sat together on a fur Laki had spread out, while Klamro and Nerto squatted down with their backs to the sea.

Once the beer bowl was circulating, Heln began the talk. "How are you finding Cow Village, Bokka? Has it changed much with the death of Genu?"

Klamro answered slowly, considering. "Yes, there have been changes. Genu was difficult sometimes, but he usually explained what he wanted. He told us all about the tomb he wanted to build, that kind of thing. Pru's way of leading the village is leaving lots of work not done."

"She doesn't want us to go hunting or fishing until Genu is buried," Nerto explained. "We're looking after the cows and the sheep, and we're doing some of the basic work in the fields, but we're not bringing in the food from the shore and the woods which we'd usually have."

"That's probably why she doesn't want visitors," Klamro added. "Her father would have thrown a feast for you. You know he was generous, perhaps too generous, with those things, and would have had us hunting for deer every day if visitors stayed for a while. But Pru's told us *no hunting, only tomb building*, and she can't stick to that and do what she sees as her duty to visitors."

"So she decided to be rude to us instead." Heln didn't sound hurt, but ey clearly wanted it stated.

"And then to come and bully Bokka." Nerto was looking at eir daughter, but Bokka didn't look back. Instead, she took the stone ball out from her pouch and started work on it. "When Pru had turned you away, she followed Bokka—and told her off for coming back to her own home village. Bokka had come to find us, grazing the sheep in a clearing at the edge of the woods, and Pru yelled at her in front of us."

"Sounds horrible," Laki whispered to Bokka.

Bokka didn't reply but handed Laki the stone ball. Turning it in her hand, Laki could see that it was almost finished. The dent where Jeko had thrown it had vanished into the design, and only one knob now needed finishing and smoothing.

"Will you polish it, or leave the surface like this?" Laki asked. She kept her voice very soft so that she didn't interrupt what Heln was saying.

"Leave it," Bokka said, equally quietly. "Too smooth and shiny isn't so nice to feel."

Laki could see that. The sandstone had a warmth and satisfaction to it in the smooth but unpolished state left by Bokka's pecking with another stone. "Good idea." She handed the ball back to Bokka and risked another question. "What do you want to do next?"

Bokka sighed, and now she did glance over towards Nerto, who was explaining something to Heln with a series of bold gestures. "I suppose we can't run away and hide in the woods forever."

"Probably not," Laki agreed. The volume of their conversation had risen slightly—Bokka had forgotten to keep her voice down when she lifted her head—and when Nerto finished talking, the other four all turned to look at Laki and Bokka. Laki put her arm around Bokka's shoulders. "What are our options?" she asked.

They all started to speak at once. Bokka held up her hand and they stopped.

"Nerto first," Laki said.

"You could stay here," Nerto said. "We could call a village meeting and try and get a new leader chosen. People won't stand for the way Pru is behaving much longer, anyway. There probably isn't time to build you a new house before the winter, not when we need to finish the tomb, but we do extend the village sometimes. By this time next year, the two of you could be set up together and have a full role in Cow Village. I know Laki has lots of useful skills, and we've already been missing Bokka's work on stone carving and wheat grinding and lots of other things."

Ey spun an attractive picture in some ways, but Laki wasn't as confident as Nerto about the change in leadership. And Klamro—perhaps seeing her doubt—was ready to put forward another idea.

"You don't have to commit to that all at once," ey said. "You could stay here for a little while, perhaps until after the funeral, and then move on again."

"How would we leave?" Laki asked. "Heln and Marko can't stay, even if you can talk people into accepting me as well as Bokka."

"Well, I think we could ask for them to stay for a while," Klamro said.

"Or we could come back," Heln offered. Ey gestured northwards. "We could go a bit further up the coast—we'd been thinking about that anyway, check out the next village or two and see if there's some more trading to be done this year—and when we turned round, we could come back past here and ask you whether you wanted to leave again."

"I suppose I could go with you," Laki said, but Bokka clutched at her arm.

"Only if I'm coming with you," Bokka said. That at least was clear. Laki turned to give her a smile, and Bokka gave her a kiss instead.

Heln cleared eir throat. "Or if you want to leave, you can come with us. We could go on northwards to a few more villages, or straight back to Otter Village."

"I think if you keep going north, you'll find that the coast turns east," Nerto said. "You wouldn't have to come back here. You could keep going around the coast and you'd find you'd gone all the way around the island. No need to worry about us and coming back if you've taken both of them with you."

"So you could come back to Otter Village," Marko said. "I know there are some people there who are difficult, but isn't that the case anywhere?"

"It certainly is here," Klamro said, "And in the village I grew up in, and the one my sister moved to, and..."

"Yes, we get the idea," Bokka said. She scowled at her parent. "I know people are difficult everywhere, but the question here isn't about them. It's about what I want to do with my life."

"True," Klamro acknowledged with a little tilt of eir head. "So, what do you want to do?"

"I don't know."

"You have always had different ideas to other people," Nerto said. "I think you could do all sorts of things...whatever you want to do. I think you could make a new kind of life. I think you could make stone balls and axe-heads and all sorts of useful and lovely things, and Heln could help you trade them, and you could have a good life from that."

Bokka was nodding along, and Klamro asked, "Does that sound like the sort of life you want? Are we looking for a place where you can do that?"

"I don't know," Bokka said again. She looked down and suddenly seemed sad or stuck on some unpleasant thought. Laki put her arm around Bokka's shoulders and hugged her.

"You need time to decide," Marko observed. "You've got until the morning, at the very least."

"And maybe longer," Heln said. "We'll need to wait for the tide, and it probably won't be until a while after dawn. We might have to wait for more than that if this wind doesn't turn. It was good for coming into the beach, but it would be difficult to launch into."

"So you can take your time," Marko said. "I think we should rest, if we can. Do you want to sleep out here, or go into the village?"

"We'll go into the village," Nerto said, standing up. "My old bones are too stiff for sleeping on the beach when there's a warm house in there."

Laki assumed at first that Bokka would go with them, and she let Bokka go to allow her to stand up and leave with her parents. But Bokka didn't move away. "I'll stay here," she said. "Goodnight."

"We'll come at dawn to see you," Klamro said. Ey took Nerto's hand. "At dawn you can tell us whether you want to stay, or stay for a while, or go, or something else. You'll have the night to think. And whatever you choose, we'll try and help you, whether that means telling Pru that you're both staying, or bringing you food for the journey."

Bokka nodded, as if this was simply what she expected. "Thank you," Laki said, because she thought that Bokka's parents were being surprisingly generous. They were the ones who would suffer most, she guessed, if Bokka left and never came back, or if the village got into a conflict about the leadership and who could live there or not.

Once Nerto and Klamro had left, taking with them a burning branch from the fire to light their way, Heln and Marko said they would settle down to sleep next to the boat where they could put a skin up as a tent above them, stretched out from the side of the boat. "You two can stay on the grass up there," Heln said. "You'll be warm enough in your furs." The spot ey indicated was a little further from the fire than Laki had been thinking of sleeping, but it was soft grass and would be nicer in that regard.

"I expect they'll keep each other warm," Marko added. His hand touched Heln's lower back and he grinned.

"There are always options with two," Heln replied. Ey and Marko left to sort out their own sleeping arrangements.

Bokka shook out some furs which had been rolled up, and she and Laki made a kind of nest. They settled down, facing each other. Laki thought they had put their backs to the world and made a little new life of sorts in this tiny space between them.

*

The stars were clear and bright. Laki had rolled away slightly and was sleeping on her back, with a tiny snore now and then. From the other side of the boat, Bokka could hear a louder snore which she guessed was Marko.

She wasn't sleeping anymore and her bladder was full, so she stood up. She took a fur with her and pulled it around her shoulders. When she'd pissed, she came back to where Laki was sleeping, intending to lie down again herself, but it didn't feel right.

Last night, it had felt so good to be close to Laki. Close enough to kiss, close enough to touch, close enough to orgasm. So close that for a moment she had thought they might never separate. Standing in the starlight, though, she felt very distant from Laki again. Whatever Laki was doing in her sleep—whatever she was dreaming—Bokka couldn't be part of it. She looked at Laki's necklace, which was white enough to reflect some extra light and glow against Laki's brown skin. She remembered wanting the necklace. Having it, in fact.

She couldn't take it now without waking Laki. What would it even mean to take it from her, when Laki had declared her intention of finding a way to live with Bokka?

What would it mean for them to be together?

Bokka tucked the furs around Laki and picked up her belt with the pouches on. She squeezed one to make sure her stone ball was still in there. She couldn't work on it here; it would be too loud and wake people. She walked away, following the curve of the shore towards the woods.

She hadn't intended to go far, but she wasn't sure how far the sound would carry on a quiet night. The tide was out, and the sound of waves was soft and more distant than it had been. She ended up walking into the woods, and then out into a clearing above the cliffs, before she felt she was far enough away not to worry about disturbing the sleepers.

There wasn't enough light to really see her work, so she pecked at the ball by feel, spending more time running her fingertips over the surfaces than knocking away tiny chips with her hammerstone. She gave it one or two strikes, felt it, struck again; but it was almost finished, and it was difficult to perfect it. Each strike took more thinking time now.

Somewhere behind her, the dawn was coming. Fewer stars were visible. The sky lightened into a deep blue and then a pale grey. Bokka wondered what was going to happen. Would she and Laki leave here today?

Did she want to? It was up to her, at least in part. That felt like a surprise—how many things in life were really her own choice?—but also like a kind of power. If she wanted to stay, she could simply stay. She could even stay up here, watching the light changing over the sea, hearing the tree branches rattle as a breeze went past, being alone if she wanted to or with nobody but Laki.

They could build a little house up here, all their own. There was plenty of stone nearby, and she could make an axe and cut down a tree and split it into timbers to support the roof, and thatch it with bundles of rushes from the edge of the stream, and eat the roots, and when it was ready she would go to Laki—who had somehow been waiting by the boat the whole time— and say, "Come and live with me. I have a house for two people and we can live there without anyone bothering us."

And Laki would probably laugh and ask where their wheat would come from and what about the sheep and all those sorts of things. Bokka scowled at the sea. The soil was too thin for fields up here and they would have to have sheep from the flock in Cow

Village, who would probably wander back to Klamro all the time because ey was their favourite human.

It was truly dawn now. Bokka wondered whether the others had woken, but she couldn't see the boat from here and she didn't want to go and check. They would ask her what she wanted to do. If she told them, they would laugh at her as the imaginary Laki had done.

She found another stone with potential and starting roughing out an axe-head. Perhaps she couldn't build a house, but she could make something useful. And for the time being—until someone came to fetch her and tell her what to do next—she could be alone.

Chapter 14

KLAMRO SHOOK LAKI'S SHOULDER. "Hello, hello."

"Ugh?"

"We've come to hear the decision," Klamro said. "What are you going to do? Are you and Bokka staying?"

"Dunno." Laki struggled to sit up; she had wrapped the furs so tightly around herself she could hardly move. And something was missing. She touched her neck, and the necklace was still there. Bokka. Where was Bokka?

The light was bright, but she forced herself to look around. Klamro, very close – ey'd woken her. Nerto, a few paces away. The boat. Heln and Marko's voices, not quite close enough to make out what they were saying, but not far away.

"The tide has turned but it'll be a while before it's high enough to launch the boat easily," Nerto said, "so you've got some time to work it out. Where's Bokka, anyway?"

Good question.

"She was here," Laki said, patting the furs beside her as if Bokka could have become completely flat and hidden between them. "She was sleeping..."

But she wasn't there now, and her cloak wasn't there, and one of the furs was gone, too.

"She probably went to piss or something." Nerto was brisk, reassuring.

"I hope she didn't go too far." Klamro turned to look back towards the village, perhaps hoping to see her, perhaps worrying that Pru or someone else might be coming to investigate.

"Did you decide what to do?" Nerto asked.

Laki shook her head, which made her feel dizzy. She squatted down again to wait for it to pass. "We talked a bit last night but..." They'd been distracted, feeling the joy of their bodies rather than worrying about the future. "It's not easy to know what would be best."

Heln and Marko appeared. Marko immediately started refreshing the fire, which had burnt down to embers but was still hot in the centre. "We'll eat, and then you can tell us what you want to do, and whoever is sailing away can leave," Heln said to Laki.

"If we know what we want to do," Laki said. She felt quite despairing suddenly. Perhaps they would be stuck on this beach forever, not knowing whether to force their way into Cow Village or try and make a life in Otter Village.

"Here." Nerto handed Laki a strip of dried meat. "It's beef."

"Thank you." Laki chewed slowly.

"You'll work it out," Klamro said. "Bokka takes her time, sometimes, to decide what she wants—you'll have seen her searching a whole beach for exactly the right pebble to use as a hammer, and once when she was first old enough to go out to the woods alone she spent a whole day deciding what to wear on her hunting trip—but she gets there."

"I think I hurried her." Laki felt guilty, remembering how she had encouraged Bokka to leave Cow Village and pressured her with the thought that the boat would be leaving soon—one chance and never again.

"Maybe." But Klamro smiled at her. "And maybe not. She can't usually be hurried into something she doesn't want to do. Believe me, I've tried to get her to come and help with the sheep when she didn't want to be near them."

Nerto snorted, which made Laki think there must be more to the story.

"I'm going to fetch some more water," Marko announced. "We might as well make porridge if we'll be waiting a while."

"Not that long, for the tide," Heln said.

"We have to wait until Bokka's ready to decide."

"Laki, we have to leave as soon as we can," Heln replied. Eir voice was gentle but firm—*ey'd learned that trick from Trebbi,* Laki thought. "We told Pru that we would go. We can't wait for too long, because if she finds us still here, she might ask us to leave in a hurry."

"But—"

"So," Heln continued, "you'll have to find Bokka, and the two of you will have to decide."

"Won't Bokka be back soon?" Laki asked. Surely she wasn't far away.

Klamro looked around, but Nerto shrugged. "You can never tell with Bokka."

"Should I go and look for her?"

"No need, she'll come when she's ready," Klamro said, but Heln said, "Yes—we can't be waiting for her when it's time to go."

Laki looked between the two of them. Klamro was Bokka's parent and had known Bokka her whole life. Heln was in charge of the boat and eir word would be the final one on anything to do with the launch. Laki tried to imagine Bokka. Going to piss and not wanting to come back? Going to find something and getting distracted? Going...and not knowing whether she should come back, not knowing whether Laki wanted her there, worrying that she was causing trouble, wanting to stay and not knowing how to say it to Laki?

"Wait for us," Laki said, thinking of the spot on the cliff they had visited before. "I'll look for her. Actually, I think I know where she'll be."

Heln nodded. Laki didn't look at Nerto and Klamro but set off at a brisk pace.

*

Bokka heard movement and glanced round before Laki came into sight.

"There you are!"

"Here I am."

"I was worried," Laki said.

"Why?"

"Well, I woke up—in fact, your parents woke me up—and I didn't know where you were."

Bokka had forgotten about Klamro and Nerto coming at dawn. She started to stand up, but Laki waved her down again. "They weren't as worried as I was." Laki gestured towards the fur Bokka was sitting on. "May I join you for a bit?"

"Are we hiding here?"

"I suppose so." Laki sat down so close that Bokka could feel the warmth of her skin. It wasn't a big fur. Laki was warm from walking up the hill. "We have to decide what to do."

"I know," Bokka said. She expected Laki to continue, but instead there was a silence. "I know we need to decide. I don't feel ready, though. I don't want to leave here forever, or live in Otter Village forever, but I don't know what else we can do."

"We don't have to decide about forever." Laki took Bokka's hand. "We only have to decide about this summer. And we don't have to decide it all at once. All we have to decide for today is...today. Do you want to stay in Cow Village today? Do I want to stay in Cow Village today? That means arguing with Pru, I think, but your parents seem to think they could win. I'm not sure if it's harder or easier if it's both of us. Or if we don't want to stay, do we want to go north and find some more villages, places neither of us have ever been, or south and work our way back towards Otter Village? Or stop somewhere on the way?"

Bokka knew all that. It wasn't the point.

"It's up to us," Laki added. "Just you and me, choosing what to do—we're not going to go to any meetings. We're just going to listen to ourselves and Goddess here and now." She stroked her thumb over the back of Bokka's hand. "What do you want?"

Bokka didn't know. She didn't even know how to work out what she wanted.

"What do *you* want?" she asked in the end.

Laki sighed. Bokka wondered what she'd done wrong; was it not supposed to include Laki, this decision which would affect both of them?

"I want to be with you," Laki said. That surprised Bokka enough to make her glance up. She met Laki's eyes for an instant before looking away. Laki's eyes had been wide, the way people sometimes were when they were startled. "I love you and I want to spend my life with you. As soon as we met, I was interested in you, before I even knew who you were, and we've connected more strongly than I've ever felt before. That has to be Goddess work, making the world the way it is."

Laki loves me. She thinks Goddess brought us together. Bokka's heart beat hard. It wasn't answering the question, though. "But *where* do you want to spend your life? Goddess didn't give us a magic village where everyone is lovely."

"Well, I want to be somewhere we can both be happy," Laki said. "And only if you want that, too."

"I want that." Bokka squeezed Laki's hand, hoping that she could transmit her desires and her longings that way, as her feelings had seemed fully expressed through touch the night before. "But I don't know what that means. What do we do?"

Laki replied only in an answering squeeze. A particularly loud wave crashed below them and Bokka looked out to sea. The tide was rising.

"Heln will want to leave soon," she said.

"Yes." Laki turned to her. "Bokka, maybe it doesn't matter where we go. There doesn't seem to be a right thing to do. If we stay, if we go, if we travel, if we start a new village...it's all going to be difficult. It's all going to involve at least some other people, and some disagreements and some challenges. So I think it doesn't matter what we choose for today. We can stay here—in Cow Village, I mean, or even on this exact spot. We can run down and go with Heln. As long as we do it together, that will be the best we can do."

Stay together with Laki. Go here or there, but always with the same person. Always with Laki. It was a good thought. Bokka pictured a few situations: grinding wheat alongside Laki; picking berries next to Laki; going to the beach alone but bringing the crabs she found back home to Laki; sailing from one village to the next, in a little boat, with only just enough space for herself and Laki and some supplies.

"Yes," she said. She lifted her hand, the one Laki was holding, to Laki's face, and stroked her cheek with their joined hands. "We'll stay together."

"You'll stay nearby?" Laki asked. "I know you need to spend time on your own, but come to a place like this, where I know where to look for you."

"Of course." Laki was so good at finding her, Bokka didn't think this needed to be said, but she didn't want to argue with Laki at the moment. "And you'll stay—even if we stay in Cow Village, you'll argue with Pru and try to get her to let you stay?"

"Whatever I need to do." Laki turned her head to press a kiss to the palm of Bokka's hand. "I'll do whatever I need to do to stay here, if that's what we choose to do. Pru deserves to be argued with, anyway."

Bokka chuckled. "I've often tried." She used the hand which was now cupping Laki's chin to pull her in for a proper kiss.

Bokka had expected a short kiss and more conversation, but Laki opened her mouth and pulled Bokka close, and somehow they tipped over and were lying, side by side, on the furs, and kissing and kissing. Bokka was very aware of her tongue, and the taste of Laki—the taste of dried meat in Laki's mouth. When Laki moved back slightly, panting, Bokka asked, "Did you eat Nerto's dried beef this morning?"

Laki nodded.

"It's making my mouth water."

Smiling, Laki propped herself up on one elbow. "You must be hungry."

"Yes."

"And the others will be waiting for us." Laki waved a hand. "Not that it matters. They can wait or do whatever they want. If Heln and Marko sail away without us, we'll stay here until they come back or some other traders arrive. Not a problem. But if you want to go down, we can find you something to eat."

"But I like kissing you."

Laki leaned in and Bokka kissed her again, not so deeply now, short and gentle.

"I know," Laki said. "We'll have plenty of time for that. We're going to spend our whole lives together, remember?"

That didn't do much to make Bokka think that they should stop kissing now, but she saw Laki's point. And she was hungry, now she'd remembered that food existed.

"Our whole lives for kissing," she told Laki.

"Our whole lives." Laki smiled at her until the contact seemed too intense and Bokka had to look away, stand up, and fold up the fur. They went down towards the beach hand in hand.

*

They didn't talk much on the way. Bokka seemed deep in thought and Laki felt that she had said what needed saying.

As they came in sight of the beach, though, Laki asked, "Who's that?"

The boat was still there—which was a relief, despite her earlier attempt at bravery. If Heln and Marko had really left without waiting for her, she would have felt abandoned. Marko stood by the cooking fire. In front of him, Klamro and Nerto were facing three other people.

Bokka ran through what she could see. After naming her parents, she went on to say, "And Pru is there, and Storna, and Nodos."

Laki didn't even recognise the last name. "Why would they have come?"

"I've no idea."

"We'll find out when we get there," Laki said. As they walked on, Bokka's fingers brushed Laki's wrist, and she turned her hand so that Bokka could grasp it. "That's right. We'll arrive together and we'll stay together, whatever they say." Laki tried to work out for herself what might be happening. Pru could be enforcing the rule she'd made last night, that the boat had to leave this morning. Or she could be arguing with Nerto and Klamro—they seemed to be opposing her. Or maybe she was making some other claim—that Cow Village had to be given gifts in return for the use of their beach, or something. Those things should have been said at their arrival, but Laki thought Pru was the sort of person who would try and make new rules later when it suited her.

"If you do that," Klamro was saying as Laki and Bokka got closer, "not only will we let our daughter leave with these people, as you put it, we'll go as well. People have to be free to make partnerships, Pru, and trade, and move between villages when they want to."

"You can leave if you like," Pru said sulkily. She crossed her arms and hunched her shoulders. "I don't care. You don't really support Cow Village anyway."

Klamro laughed. "I don't support Cow Village? Really? When I spend more time caring for our sheep than anyone else in the village, when I'm out in the fields night and day at lambing time, when Nerto hardly sees me because our flocks have grown so much?"

"So if you care for the sheep so much, why did one go missing?" Pru shot back.

"If I didn't care for the sheep so much, it wouldn't have come back to me so easily," Klamro replied.

"Well, you can't take them with you."

Klamro opened eir mouth, with an absolutely furious expression, and Laki thought ey might have been about to explain a plan to do exactly that—to steal all the sheep and leave Cow Village with none. But ey caught sight of Bokka arriving in that moment and shut eir mouth again. Laki was glad. Coming into this sort of situation was difficult enough, and shouting might be enough to make Bokka run away.

And if she did, Laki would go with her. The force of that new commitment struck her hard, and she looked to Marko and Heln hoping that they would support her.

166

Heln caught her eye and gave her a nod. Ey might not know everything which was happening, but ey was on her side.

Marko was watching Pru intently. It wasn't really a rejection of Laki, though, because Pru had taken advantage of Klamro's silence to start listing reasons why Nerto and Klamro should leave—all sorts of petty grievances which seemed to go back for years. "... and you don't keep your daughter under control," she was saying, "and you let her steal things and you didn't bring a fair share of bread to the midwinter feast..."

"Because our roof leaked and your father wouldn't help us repair it and our grain grew mould," Nerto said, not quite a mutter but quietly enough that Pru simply continued talking over em.

"... and you spend all that time with the sheep and don't help with the children of the village and you always argue when we have village meetings and you aren't helping enough with my father's tomb and..." Pru paused, almost sobbing, a tear rolling down her cheek. Laki felt a little sympathy for her—she was only the same age as Laki, pushed into being the village leader, mourning her father, and maybe she felt very alone and scared in that situation.

"Yes, and you're lazy and ugly and your house smells of sheep shit," Nodos added. Laki rapidly revised her view of Pru, who had chosen her friends and come into this confrontation on purpose.

"And you," Nerto said, "are not fit to be a leader." Eir voice was still quieter than Pru's, but now it was firm and clear. Ey looked directly at Pru, ignoring Nodos and her insults. "I'm sorry you've been put in this position. Your father died, and we all miss him. But you are too young, or too selfish, or something, and you are not acting for the good of the village."

"Oh yeah?" Pru said, leaning forward. "And what are you going to do about it?"

"Call a village meeting and have someone else chosen as leader."

Next to Nerto, Klamro nodded. "We should have had a village meeting before now, anyway."

"It's for the leader to decide when we have a meeting. You can't decide to do that!" Pru said, but Storna was frowning, and Laki could see that Nerto was on firm ground.

She also realised that she and Bokka had been almost completely forgotten. The argument might have been started by Bokka's leaving and returning, but that was now a tiny grain of sand in a whole jar of flour.

"Come this way," Laki whispered to Bokka, tugging on her hand.

Not moving too fast, not making a fuss, simply leaving; Laki managed to lead Bokka away without trying to hide but also without attracting any attention. Heln glanced over briefly before turning back to listen to what Nerto was now saying to Pru.

Once they were by the remains of Marko's cooking fire, and far enough away that soft voices wouldn't be heard—especially when some other people were shouting—Laki said, "Would you like to eat? There's some bread left from the other day, or we could light the fire again..."

"Some bread," Bokka said, helping herself from the top of Heln's pack. Laki picked up a jar and discovered that it had been refilled with fresh water, too—probably intended for the journey, but it could be filled again. She offered it to Bokka, but Bokka was already strolling a little further along the shore, head down to look for something.

"Ah!" She squatted to pick a handful of marsh samphire, the bright green leaves swollen with salty water. She passed some to Laki.

"How long do you think that will go on?" Bokka asked when they'd each eaten a little.

"Until they work something out, I guess."

"What do we do?"

"Whatever we like." Laki looked at Bokka, who held out her hand. Laki took it.

"Do you think we should listen and find out what they're deciding?"

"If you want to," Laki said, "but when they decide, they can come and tell us the answer. I think we only really need to listen if we want to join in with the discussion." She remembered something that Trebbi would say. "The point of going to a village meeting is to help Goddess help everyone, right? So we go if we think Goddess might use us to help the others make a decision."

Bokka considered that. "Genu didn't talk about Goddess like that. I don't think Goddess uses me to talk to other people."

"Maybe She can send her messages another way," Laki suggested.

"Through someone else?"

"Well, yes. But also not only through speaking. The things we do, the choices we make..."

"You mean we might be sending them," Bokka's hands were full of pebbles she was picking up from the beach, so she tipped her head to indicate the little crowd of arguers, "a message from Goddess by refusing to join in with the argument."

"Maybe." Laki actually wasn't sure at all, since in Otter Village people were mostly very happy with their village meetings and came along without a fuss, but it made a certain sense. She could hope.

"So do we do anything else?"

"Only if we want to," Laki said. "Or only if Goddess guides us to."

Bokka thought about that. She made her beach pebbles into a little conical pile, with one balanced on top pointing to the sky. "I only feel that I want to be near you and away from them."

"Then that's what we'll do."

Bokka nodded. "Shall we find some food while we wait?"

Chapter 15

THEY COLLECTED A FEW LIMPETS BUT neither of them were really hungry. After a while Bokka said, "Let's go into the woods instead." She saw Laki glance over at the conversation still in progress. Pru was yelling now, full on yelling from the bottom of her lungs, and there was no way Bokka wanted to go near that.

"They're going to be a while," Laki concluded. She put the stone on which they had gathered the limpets down by the high water mark—probably the limpets would simply cling there until they got back—and gestured, a wide sweep of the hand which Bokka thought meant *lead on.*

"This way."

They left the beach and walked south, away from the village and the shouting and the cliffs. Instead, Bokka took them through the fields towards the forest. One or two people were working and paused to greet her.

"I didn't know you were back." Aiso's son had been weeding around clumps of beans until he straightened up to speak to them.

"I might not be here for long," Bokka explained, although he still looked puzzled.

"Well, welcome for as long as you stay."

"Thanks." Bokka kept walking. She hoped Aiso's son would stop staring at them soon and go back to his work. At least she could hear Laki's footsteps close behind.

She held out a hand and Laki took it. They reached the edge of the fields and Bokka looked around. She used to use an entrance to the path through the woods here, between two elms which grew close together, but it was almost overgrown with nettles.

"Over there?" Laki asked. It was. The new entrance was wider, suitable for taking large stones through. Bokka didn't like the change but she could see why it had happened. And it suggested they were going the right way.

In the woods, Bokka saw more signs. The path had been heavily used. It had been widened and flattened to take the rollers which carried the largest stones. Before long, they came into a clearing which had once been quiet, a spot where deer grazed and the sunlight fell dappled through the trees. Now it was much used and a few people were working, even though they would normally be with the crops or the flocks. The ground was churned to mud. In the centre, a stone building was rising. A stack of large, flat stones stood to one side, ready to form the roof when the walls had been built.

"So he chose the upright stones as dividers in the end," Laki said. Bokka was impressed—she hadn't realised Laki had listened so carefully to the endless debates which had been happening, not so long ago, about the design which should be used for the tomb.

"Well, we chose them." Teni emerged from behind a pile of small stones. Her face and hair were grey with dust. "Genu actually died before the decision was made, but when Pru said it had to be finished for his body, we picked the one which would be quickest to build with what we've got and got on with it."

"We can help," Bokka said.

Teni gave them some basic jobs to do—Laki to sort stones from the pile and carry them to Bokka, who would lay them into the mound which was forming around the core of the tomb. "We don't want them to slip," Teni explained, "so try and arrange them so they're fitted together."

Laki asked some questions and learned that the roof of the tomb would hopefully be added later today. "We're waiting for Pru to come and confirm the exact arrangement of stones," Teni said.

"That might not happen." Bokka carried on laying stones, although she noticed Laki stopped bringing them over in favour of explaining the situation.

"What do you think we should do?" Teni asked.

"It's not for me to say," Laki said. "I don't even live in this village."

"We'd better find someone to ask."

"You might want to go to the village meeting."

"But we need to finish."

Bokka put down the last stone of the set Laki had brought and stepped back from the half–built tomb. "Genu's dead. I think his body can wait another day."

There was a pause. "Can it?" Laki asked.

Teni sighed. "Perhaps. No, not really. We put him up in one of the trees, away from the ground, but of course the birds come..."

"Some people used to be buried like that," Bokka observed.

"I know. Pru said it was better than the water, anything other than the water for Genu. But what he really wanted was the tomb and we all know that."

Bokka looked around the clearing. The tomb was much more complete than the last time she'd seen it, when only a few key stones had been in place. "If we put the roof on," she said, "there'll only be the mound to finish." The slabs of stone for the roof were too large for two people, but the mound would be easy enough. "Pru isn't coming. If you help us put the roof on now, Laki and I can finish the rest while you go to the village meeting."

"Pru might be upset."

"Pru already is upset," Laki said, "because the village isn't going to have her as the leader anymore. Finishing the tomb at least means she'll know her father was buried properly."

"What if she is still leader and she says we should have waited?"

Laki hesitated. Bokka watched her thinking, looking from Teni to the half–finished tomb and back again, her hands opening and closing. It was hard to resist touching those hands, giving them something to hold even while the tomb couldn't be completed.

"Teni!"

Someone was running down the path. Teni turned. "Storna!"

"Come quickly, we're having a meeting, and—" Storna paused, seeing Bokka and Laki for the first time. "What are you doing here? You should be waiting by the boat until you're told to leave! Or going already!"

"We're helping with the tomb," Bokka said, fetching another stone for the mound.

"Yes, Storna, what do you think we should do?" Teni asked. "Pru wanted to come and tell us how to arrange the stones for the roof, but apparently she might not be able to come."

"You'd better come and see what's happening," Storna said. "I was sent to fetch you."

"Never mind what's happening at the village," Bokka whispered to Laki. "We should get on with it. Let's get the roof stones on."

"It'll be too heavy for us."

Bokka wanted to have a go, but Laki was probably right. "They should help us before they leave."

"What are you two whispering about?" Storna asked in exactly the way Pru used to—as if she had a right to know everything Bokka thought.

"Never mind," Bokka muttered, but Laki said calmly, "We'd be happy to keep working on the tomb while you deal with things back at the village. If you could help us lift the roof slabs into place..."

She went over towards the pile and touched the first slab. Storna and Teni moved towards her as if it was obvious—as if Teni had forgotten all her objections to starting this part of the work. Why would they do that?

Whatever caused it, Bokka liked the result. She watched them carry two, then three slabs and place them over the uprights to form a tunnel in the centre of the tomb.

"You could help, too," Laki said as she passed Bokka on the way back for the fourth slab. True. Bokka went to carry another corner, and the next three slabs came even more quickly.

"Do we need another one?" Storna asked, pointing to the slight gap at the end of the tunnel.

"I think it's okay," Laki said. "Anyway, Bokka and I will work on the mound from the back, and you can add another roof slab later, before it's finished, if you want to."

"Thank you," Teni said. She tried to brush stone dust and mud out of her hair, but with very little success. Bokka passed her a drinking skin which still had some water in. Bokka would have hated to have so much dirt on her face even for that long. "I really had better go and see what's happening in the village. Storna, if Pru isn't going to be our leader anymore, who is?"

It wouldn't matter. Bokka turned away as they walked out of the clearing and went back to the stones. Piling up the mound wasn't too difficult; it was a matter of bringing stones from the bags which had been used to collect them and stacking them in such a way that they didn't fall or roll away. As she selected each stone, she rolled it in her hands to quickly understand its full shape, then looked for a space on the mound where it would fit without moving.

Laki put a few in, then one tumbled and took some others with it.

"You have to place them carefully." Bokka demonstrated.

"I don't think I'll ever be that good," Laki said. "Mine always roll away. It's okay—you work on the mound. I'll bring you the stones."

They settled into a rhythm easily, with Laki providing a steady stream of choices, and Bokka feeling each one and finding the right place for it. There were one or two small falls, but very few. The mound grew steadily and started to cover the roof stones. The sun rose and started to fall in the sky.

"Are you tired?" Laki asked eventually.

Bokka shook her head. She placed the stone she was holding just so, and straightened up. The first three roof stones were now entirely covered, and she was standing on the base of the mound in order to reach up that high.

"Well, I am." Laki swung her arms and stretched them over her head.

"I thought you wanted to finish this?"

"I do, but I'm going to need a break. And maybe something to eat, and some water." She'd paused to chew on a couple of roasted hazelnuts from her pouch, but there wasn't any water in the clearing, and she didn't have her drinking skin with her. Noticing this, Bokka realised that Laki probably did need a rest.

"We can sit for a bit." There was a fallen tree at one side of the clearing and the trunk, although sloping slightly, made a good seat. "There's so much more to do."

174

"Yes," Laki said, but Bokka saw her looking along the tomb, assessing progress. "We've done a lot of work, though. Remember how it was when we arrived?"

*

They stayed in Cow Village for the funeral. Heln wasn't at all sure, saying that surely the people of Cow Village would want to be on their own, but Bokka wanted to stay and that meant Laki wanted to stay, and when she explained this to Heln, ey came around. They all helped with the tomb, mucking in to make sure it was finished, and that helped, too.

Laki thought she knew what to expect at a funeral. She'd been to several, including her mother's. She expected lots of silence, and some tears, and some words to the ancestors.

In Cow Village, they did things differently. Genu's body was fetched from the tree where it had been resting, and bundled up in leather, and tied shut—where Laki's people would normally have left him in his clothes. "It hardly looks like a body," Bokka whispered when the bundle came past.

They paraded through the fields and the woods to the tomb. In Otter Village, they would have gone quietly. Laki remembered hearing the cries of gulls and an eagle on the way to her mother's funeral. In Cow Village, it was impossible to hear anything but the wailing of the people. Pru started it, with great sobbing cries. The others copied.

Fortunately, Bokka and Laki were already near the back. Bokka tugged at Laki's hand, and they walked more slowly, falling further behind until the sound wasn't so loud. "I'd forgotten," Bokka said.

"I didn't know," Laki replied.

When they were finally all gathered around the tomb, there was a little bit of silence. Pru gave a long talk about everything Genu had done in his life, stressing all the benefits of having him as leader, talking about all the work he'd put into the tomb. People responded to each point with cries of agreement, shouts of loss, and support for Pru.

"He didn't do that much work on the tomb," Bokka said at one point – fortunately only into Laki's ear. "He did a lot of talking about it. We did much more building."

Laki nodded but didn't risk a reply. Someone might have overheard them and it wasn't the moment.

With more noise and ceremony, Pru took Genu's body into the tomb. "He is in the most important place, right at the east end, where all the future generations will look towards him," she announced when she came out. Then she took in offerings for him and items to represent his own ancestors: a felted doll for his mother and her mother, a joint of meat cut from the cow they had killed to roast later, and handfuls of summer flowers. She announced and explained each one at length. Next to Laki, Bokka shifted from foot to foot, and reached into her pouch to touch her finished stone ball several times. They'd agreed that it wouldn't be right to start polishing it at the funeral, but Bokka was clearly tempted.

When Pru finally finished taking things into the tomb, they covered the entrance with some wooden boards to temporarily prevent anyone else from entering. Laki hoped there might finally be some silence—she wanted to spend at least a little time with Goddess if she was to properly acknowledge the burial of Genu— but instead the people sang. It started as a wordless tune. Bokka hummed along. Gradually, people added words to it, improvising verses which spoke of Genu's role in their lives or something he had done.

It was clever. Against all her instincts, Laki realised that it was also close to Goddess. She could feel Her moving in the singers as Goddess would move the speakers at an Otter Village meeting. Tears began to fall from her eyes. With a worried frown, Bokka pulled her into a hug. She wiped the tears away and smiled to reassure Bokka but couldn't explain what had happened.

*

That night at the feast, Laki set out to make it as different as possible from the ones where Bokka had been bullied before. Instead of both of them going to fetch meat, she asked Bokka to fetch bread and go and sit with Heln and Marko. "I'll go to the fire and get meat for us both." There were cooked dandelion leaves, too, which Storna told her was a tradition for funerals.

They'd nearly finished eating and Laki could see that Bokka was itching to leave when Pru came over.

Laki tensed. Her plan to make this feast different and better could all go wrong.

Pru greeted them politely, and Laki returned the greeting. Then Pru took a visible deep breath and asked, "Are you leaving tomorrow?"

So that was the line. Laki was about to reply that they didn't have to, that the new leader would decide whether they were allowed to stay or go, but before she could start speaking Bokka simply said, "Yes."

Pru nodded. "Good." She began to turn away, then glanced back. "Where are you going?"

"Wherever we want to go." Bokka's reply was immediate, where Laki would have had to think about a reasonable–sounding answer, work out how to explain their plans with some detail and not too much.

"I wish you both well."

"You too."

And Pru actually left, letting Bokka have the last word.

"That was nice of her," Bokka said softly once Pru was talking to someone else.

"I'm not sure she meant it."

Bokka shrugged. "She doesn't have to. It's enough that she has to say something nice, after all those years."

Laki would have wanted more, but she realised that this was Bokka's to choose. For a moment, she watched Bokka in the firelight; the sun had set while they ate, and the fire gave Bokka's brown skin a warm glow. Bokka wiped out her eating bowl with a crust of bread and smiled a little as she chewed.

When they first met, that exchange wouldn't have been possible. Now some of the old hurts were healing and they could spend the rest of their lives together.
"So where do you want to go?" Laki asked.

Epilogue

"WE'LL BE THERE TOMORROW," Laki reported, climbing down from the tree. "We could probably get there tonight if we kept walking—there'll be a moon."

Bokka put her pack down. "One more night without other people," she said.

Apparently that suited Laki well enough. She bent to pick up some dry wood and begin a pile of fuel for their fire. Bokka unrolled the furs they'd sleep in, found some fist sized stones to form a rough hearth, and went downhill to find the stream and fetch some fresh water. By the time she came back, Laki had used the embers she carried from last night's fire to kindle this one. She'd found some sorrel leaves they could eat with their dried meat and unpacked the last of the bread they'd been given. It was two days old, from the last village they walked through, but still good.

"In the morning we can heat some water and make porridge," she said to Bokka. "We've still got a few handfuls of oats."

Bokka nodded. She collected some more wood from beneath the trees while Laki cleaned and cut up the sorrel. The clear sky meant a cold night, and they would welcome the fire for warmth as well as cooking.

Before long, they were sitting together by the fire, eating their bread. Bokka soaked her dried meat in a little water in her eating bowl. Laki could chew it as it was, but that felt wrong to her. She realised that everything here felt okay. She wasn't anxious—perhaps a little worried about how she would cope with the noises and the people when they arrived at the market tomorrow, but not about tonight. The trees around the clearing sheltered them from the breeze, and the cool night air as the sun went down was an enjoyable contrast with the warmth of the fire in front of her, and the warmth of the cloak around her shoulders, and the warmth of Laki's body almost touching her side.

That warmth drew her. When they'd finished eating, Laki wiped out their bowls with a little water and stoked the fire. "We should leave some wood ready for the morning."

"We can keep warm another way." Bokka wasn't sure she needed to say anything, but she'd learned that Laki liked to hear a few words now and then.

"Yes." Laki came back to sit beside her, closer this time. Bokka noticed all the touches, letting her hand trail over Laki's leg, across her hip – they were pressed together there, sitting side by side. She turned towards Laki. Laki copied. Their upper bodies were face to face now. Bokka paused to look at Laki's full smiling lips, the soft skin of her neck – she stroked it with a finger, down to Laki's bone and tooth necklace. In the firelight, the bone reflected the red tones and looked on top as warm as it felt underneath, where it had absorbed the heat of Laki's body. Bokka's hand was also taking in that heat.

"Do you still want my necklace?" Laki asked, putting her hand over Bokka's where it was exploring the contrast between polished bone and smooth skin.

Bokka shook her head. "It was never the necklace I wanted." She leaned in, getting ready for a kiss. "I wanted to be close to you."

She'd said it before, but Laki liked to hear it. Laki pushed herself forward and up—Bokka wondered how until she realised Laki's arm was stretched out behind, pushing against the ground— and into Bokka's lips. They kissed long and slow. Tomorrow night, there would be people around, and they didn't have a tent as such; they might not have any time alone. Tonight, they had nothing but furs and a fire and they would not be interrupted.

Reassured by that thought, Bokka put her whole attention into the kiss. She opened her lips slightly and tasted Laki's mouth—how could it have such a distinct flavour when they had eaten exactly the same food? Nevertheless, it was sweet with the taste of Laki. Bokka licked Laki's upper lip, then the lower one, pausing when Laki's tongue met hers, but otherwise keeping to the plan.

She was distracted for another moment when Laki's hand found its way inside her tunic. It let in cool air, but she felt too warm anyway. She untied and shrugged off her cloak without taking her lips away from Laki.

"The furs are spread out behind us," Laki whispered.

Good point. Bokka lay down sideways, Laki easily coming with her, and the new angle gave her access to the base of Laki's tunic. Her hand found a snug space between the layers of leather – tunic and leggings – then snuck up inside the tunic to find the bare skin of Laki's belly.

She flattened her hand there, stroking, as she kissed Laki deeply again.

"And the same lower down, when you're ready," Laki murmured when they surfaced from the kiss.

Bokka took her time, exploring in slow circles. Here was Laki's hip, and her thigh, and her warm inner thigh; here was Laki's soft pubic hair.

"You're teasing me."

"No," Bokka said, "I'm making sure I touch everywhere," but she sped up a bit, reaching over to Laki's other side before returning to the places she thought Laki really wanted her to go.

"Kiss me as well." Laki clawed at Bokka's shoulder, pulling her down and close. Bokka pressed a finger slowly inside Laki at the same time as she reached her head forward for a kiss.

She got exactly the right place, because Laki had to let her head fall back from Bokka's lips to pant for air. "Good?" Bokka asked.

"So good, more more more," Laki replied. Bokka happily obliged.

*

Bokka woke up with her hands already moving, wanting to finish polishing one last axe-head for the market, wanting to work on the new and more intricate stone ball she was making. She did the routine things first—especially getting the fire going and the stones warming up to heat the water later—but as soon as she could, she let herself take out the leather and the sand she was using and set to work to try and get the highest possible gloss.

By the time Laki's head emerged from under the furs, Bokka had made a small but significant improvement to the axe-head. The stone was reflecting the morning sun, not enough to see details but enough to show the shape of Bokka's head as she rinsed the sand off and tipped it back and forth in her hand.

"Hello."

Bokka smiled. "The stones are hot."

"Good." Laki crawled out of bed and stretched and got herself ready for the day with a splash of cold water to her face. As Bokka had hoped, Laki got on with cooking their breakfast porridge and she was free to move on to working on her new stone ball. It was to have not the usual six but twelve knobs, each correspondingly smaller and harder to carve and more attention needed to every peck. She loved it and she loved the way that travelling alone with Laki gave her time to concentrate on it.

"This is good," she said aloud, tapping her hammerstone to start shaping a groove. "This is all going well."

"Glad to hear it." Laki put a bowl in front of her. "Food is ready."

Bokka would happily have carried on carving all morning, but the porridge would get cold. She picked up the bowl and the wooden spoon.

"We don't need to be the first to arrive," Laki said, "but if we want to get a good spot, and trade some of our axe-heads and things for the best dried meat and new skins for a tent for the winter, we'd better arrive this morning."

She assumed Laki knew. She ate her food and helped to roll up the bedding and stow everything in their packs.

It was a nice morning to walk through the woods. They found a path which one of the local villages obviously used with their cows; it led a little away from the stream and through the trees, and the sun shone, and because they didn't have to cut their way through undergrowth they could walk side–by–side. Bokka took Laki's hand.

After the birdsong and simple walking of the woods, it was a shock to come past the final trees and into fields where people were beginning to gather. The crops had been harvested and the space was open—some of it was muddy—there were a lot of people moving and shouting to each other. Bokka dropped Laki's hand, guessing that open displays of affection wouldn't be welcome, but Laki grasped it again. "We're going to stay together, and they might as well know it," she said.

They were going to stay together. Bokka focussed on memorising that as they came further into the field. Laki identified someone who seemed to be a leader and took Bokka over to introduce themselves.

"You walked?" the leader said, interested. Most people, Bokka realised, had come by boat; they had reached the place where the stream flowed out into a loch, and boats were drawn up on the shore.

"It's easier for us to gather materials and work on our stone tools as we go." Bokka thought Laki's explanation was odd because their decision had much more to do with not having time or skills or materials to make a boat, but the leader nodded and seemed happy enough. Bokka decided to follow her new rule, which was to let Laki talk to strangers.

"Well, each to their own," the leader said. "You're welcome here to trade and celebrate with us. People will be setting up tents all around here, so you can pick a spot and do whatever you like. Communal cooking over there by the village. Waste in our pit— downwind. Keep it away from the stream if you can. Trade wherever you like. Any arguments about what's worth trading for what, come to me or my partner—she's the one with the red hair and the amber pendent—or one of our sons. Despite our name, there'll be no fighting in Stag Village!"

Laki rewarded him with a laugh, and the leader moved on to deal with someone else's questions. Bokka squeezed Laki's hand.

"Where do you want to set up?" Laki asked.

Bokka pointed to the far side of the fields, where there was a slight rise and some stony ground which hadn't been planted. In between rocks, the grass was growing strongly.

"It'll be nearer the rubbish dump," Laki objected.

"And further from the people."

Laki shrugged and nodded. She let Bokka lead them over that way.

"What was the leader's name again?" Bokka asked.

"Mimna. He said it right in front of you."

"I know. I didn't remember."

They found a spot and were in the middle of unpacking their bags, laying out the axe-heads and adzes and hammers and maces, and a stone ball Bokka was ready to trade, when someone called, "Laki? Laki! Bokka!"

Startled, Bokka froze, but Laki stood up at once. "Trebbi!" They hugged, and Bokka forced herself to look up. Trebbi had been closely followed by Aleuks. There was much greeting and hugging.

"I didn't think you'd leave the village," Laki said to Trebbi when they'd covered the basics.

"Aleuks talked me into it," Trebbi said. Bokka had managed to stand. She watched the way Trebbi tipped her head towards Aleuks and smiled. Trebbi had a few grey hairs which Bokka didn't think had been there last time they met. "The village will miss me, but they still have Goddess, and plenty of good people—Dru and Heln and the others will keep things running and make sure the harvest is stored properly."

"And if you don't travel at all, you'll never know how nice it is to come home," Aleuks said. She was grinning. Trebbi didn't respond directly, so Bokka guessed this had been said a lot before.

Instead, Trebbi started asking Laki questions, and glancing at Bokka. "Who did you travel with? Will you be here for the whole celebration? Did you make these?"

"Bokka made most of them," Laki said. "I'm learning to help, and the bluish axe at the bottom is all mine. We'll stay for as long as we feel comfortable—maybe not the whole thing, I don't know. We walked here from the north; we've been exploring the coast and the woods."

"And where are you going for the winter?" Trebbi wanted to know.

Laki shrugged. Bokka wanted to be alone with Laki in the woods, and although it might not be practical in the end, Laki had agreed to try.

"We'll leave you to it," Aleuks said. Bokka felt grateful for that intervention. Maybe Aleuks had been able to tell how she felt or see that Laki couldn't answer Trebbi's question. "We're going to set up near the shore since we've got a little boat there—it's the small fishing boat, the big one is at home with Heln. You can come and find us later."

"Always," Trebbi said. As they walked away, Trebbi leaned into Aleuks' shoulder and whispered. Bokka thought it was, "They should come home with us."

She put a hand on Laki's shoulder. Laki wasn't watching the others leave—she was already back to arranging the carved stones, sorting the more practical tools from the decorative ones. "Is everything okay?" Bokka asked.

"Yes," Laki said, and looked round at Bokka. Her necklace shone in the sun; Bokka had given some of the bone beads a little extra polish. "We've got some lovely things here. We'll make some trades and be all set."

Acknowledgements

MANY THANKS TO MY WIFE, PARENTS, AND SIBLING who have supported me in thousands of ways during the creation of this book. I have explored so much of what is here—true love, religious diversity, autistic experience, nonbinary genders, and Neolithic Orkney—alongside my family that it's hard to separate my writing from our shared life. I am indebted to the members of my reading and writing groups for inspiration and feedback, especially Jo Henderson-Merrygold and Richard Clark.

Thanks to National Museums Scotland for their website and Twitter presence, and archaeologists including Hugo Anderson-Whymark who have kindly answered my questions. Laki's necklace is based on a real one found at Skara Brea, and other details about Cow Village are also based on Skara Brea. If you're in Orkney, it's a very special place to visit. Otter Village is located close to the burial place now known as the Tomb of the Otters, which is also well worth seeing if you can. I can't possibly list all the books, journals, and websites I consulted as I researched this book, but would like to thank the University of Birmingham and Birmingham City Council libraries through which I was able to access many important resources. The many archaeological errors and unfounded speculations which remain are my own. Megan Harris did excellent proofreading work for me—and any typos which remain are my own.

If you enjoyed this book…

PLEASE RATE AND REVIEW—leaving a star rating or a short comment on Goodreads, Amazon, or another website helps other readers to find this book.

I can be found on Facebook, Twitter, Mastodon, and TikTok, so come and talk to me about writing, books, religion, and life! On my blog, you can find out more about my writing and other work, and sign up to get updates by email: brigidfoxandbuddha.wordpress.com

This book also has prequel which you might enjoy:

BETWEEN BOAT & SHORE

When Aleuks arrives in Otter Village, she's looking for shelter from a storm and somewhere to trade. In Trebbi, she finds much more: a beautiful, confident woman who is serving her community and making space for love - for Aleuks. As the people of Otter Village come to terms with the death of their previous leader and work to appoint a new one, Trebbi comes into her own strength and Aleuks, previously a committed traveller, begins to realise that this is a place where she could settle down.

Order from:
https://www.amazon.co.uk/gp/product/B0B3VSCHNC/

www.ingramcontent.com/pod-product-compliance
Lightning Source LLC
Chambersburg PA
CBHW051001060726
47593CB00018B/2020